A Man Named Yuma

T. V. Olsen

THORNDIKE
CHIVERS

LIBRARY OF CONGRESS CATALOGING-IN-PUBLICATION DATA

Olsen, Theodore V.
    A man named Yuma / by T. V. Olsen.
      p. cm. — (Thorndike Press large print western)
    ISBN-13: 978-1-4104-2952-0
    ISBN-10: 1-4104-2952-0
    1. Large type books. I. Title.
    PS3565.L8M3 2010
    813'.54—dc22   2010020048

BRITISH LIBRARY CATALOGUING-IN-PUBLICATION DATA AVAILABLE
Published in 2010 in the U.S. by arrangement with Golden West Literary Agency.
Published in 2011 in the U.K. by arrangement with Golden West Literary Agency.

U.K. Hardcover: 978 1 408 49279 6 (Chivers Large Print)
U.K. Softcover: 978 1 408 49280 2 (Camden Large Print)

Printed and bound in Great Britain by the MPG Books Group
1 2 3 4 5 6 7 14 13 12 11 10

A Man Named Yuma

A Man Named Yuma

CHAPTER ONE

Yuma sat on his heels among the dun rocks at the top of the ridge, considering the place on the desert floor below him. It wasn't much, a jackleg outfit. Oily ribbons of smoke curled up from the caved-in roof whose crumbled timbers stuck up above the walls like charred jackstraws. The wooden loading platform by the south wall was smoking a little, but the fire had not spread to it.

From where Yuma was, he could see the whole layout plainly. The Store. Lando Beckett's. A low, solid, southern Arizona adobe with old wind-scarred walls whose pink-tan texture was melting back into the desert earth that rolled away flat to the east and west, ridged and wrinkled to the south and north. It was the only general supply store in a hundred or so miles either way, and it was a Haines & Harmer swing station too. Off behind it ran a river. That would be the Hidalgo, reduced to a sallow trickle by the blasting heat of midsummer.

Moving only his eyes, Yuma looked at the buzzard again. It had dropped lower now, static-winged against the gritty bronze sky. Another had joined it, wheeling in the same wide falling circle. Something, he thought, dead or near to it.

Yuma's clothes, a sweat-soiled buckskin shirt and frayed chalky jeans that clung to his catty legs and buttocks, were so worn and dull, he was nearly invisible among the dust-colored rocks. His boots were shabby and runover. His one vanity — if it could be called that — was a broad belt of smooth, beautifully tooled black leather, decorated with many alternating rows of copper studs that winked like dim fireflies when he moved, not enough to betray him by sunglare. He moved now for the first time in many minutes, raising his hand from the Sharps rifle laid across his knees to his shirt pocket. He got out a twisted coal-black Spanish cigar and stuck it in the corner of his teeth, rolling it lightly back and forth for the bitter flaky taste. It was an unusually foul brand that could be obtained only at a certain tobacconist's in Nogales — his sole use of tobacco in any form. He continued to study the layout, the deserted yard and the empty corral of ocotillo poles with the gate yawing wide open, and the smoldering ash heaps where a couple of wooden sheds had stood.

They were gone, he figured. Even if they weren't and had a reason for staying around out of sight, you'd never pick them out. It figured they were gone. Anyway he couldn't wait, and it was time for a look.

Yuma eased the Sharps off his knees and rose, taking one glance back at his rangy zebra dun standing rein-thrown in a thicket back off the skyline. He swept the tan hillside once with his eyes, then ghosted down it with a neat silent economy to his movements. He crossed the yard, not hurrying but quick and light on his feet, ready, the Sharps half-raised and held a little out from his right side. He skirted wide around the house, passing a yard from the twisted gray grid of a *ramada,* its late afternoon shadow flung long and streaky across the flinty ground. Coming around the far side of the well fifty feet from the adobe, he slowed a little because he was behind the buildings, and the willows that screened the river at this point were in sight.

He heard the moan plain enough, but took another step. He wasn't sure.

When it came again, he stopped.

Not a moan so much. More a meaty dragging gurgle, the off-tailing dregs of a pain that was no longer aware of itself.

He moved on his slow circle again, now taking his time. Then he saw it.

An adobe shed had cut off his view above and from the front yard. Keeping well out from the shed, cutting around past its mud corner, he suddenly saw the man. He was staked out, naked and spread-eagled.

Yuma moved in carefully, still not hurrying, watching everything in sight and the willows in particular. Even when he reached the man and could see him better than he wanted to, he kept half his attention on the willows and the ridgetops.

The man was gaunt, muscular, broiled red by the sun except for his burnt-leather face and hands. He had brown hair, graying, and was maybe fifty. The lids of his eyes had been cut off. The eyes were like hard-boiled eggs swimming in a jellied carnage of flesh.

They had driven four stakes into the earth in a rough square and used green rawhide to tie his wrists and ankles. That had been many hours ago. The cords had sun-shrunk and cut like wire, cutting off blood, causing his hands and feet to balloon till the toes and fingers were like discolored sausages.

Yuma squatted down, dropping the butt

10

of his rifle against the ground. It made a light thud. The man's head turned.

"Who . . . are . . . you?"

He croaked the mucky noises into words, his lidless eyes looking above Yuma's head. Sun-blinded, almost senseless. But he could still hear; the brains hadn't baked out of his head. He had been stabbed in the belly, just under the ribs and just once, so his life would hemorrhage away slowly.

Yuma pulled his knife from its buckskin sheath and cut the thongs. Even that much movement, the sudden freeing of tense-pulled muscles, made the man grunt with agony. Yuma uncapped the flat small flask he carried on his belt and let him drink, holding up his head. The man gulped mechanically, then grabbed greedily at the flask.

"Not so much. More later."

"It don't matter," the man whispered. "Plenty more water in the well."

"I didn't mean that."

"I did." His throat tissues loosened, the whisper came easier. "Look, I know. You just worry about water for you, not me. You come too late, brother, that's all. God bless you anyway."

"I'll get that hole tied off."

"Too late."

"Let's get you out of the sun first —"

Handling the man's burned body as gently as he could, Yuma moved him over a few yards to the shade of the adobe shed, then went up the hill to bring his horse down. The first thing he did was spread his ground sheet in the shade and roll the man carefully onto it. He did what he could to stop the bleeding, plugging the wound with a wad of cloth and tying a spare shirt around the man's trunk. But the man had been right, he knew. The puddle of caked darkness where he'd lain told the story: he had bled all day, his own tortured movements keeping the hole open.

"I told you it's too late," he husked. "You ought to see it now."

"Just rest easy."

"With these eyes? God, brother. You don't know. It's like they was frying inside my head."

"I know, all right."

"You know what?"

"What an Apache can do," Yuma said. "Was they Cherry-cows?"

"I think so. There was four. They —" Something worse than pain bit at his mouth. "They come in like shadows. Just after sunup. We was at breakfast and they come in the door just like that, and they had us."

"Us?"

"Beth Ann. They took me out and done what you see. They . . . they kept her in the house awhile . . . then they took her away."

"Your wife?"

"My daughter. Beth Ann." His voice began to saw irregularly up and down. "She never wanted to come here. We had a good place up north — cattle. Cool high place, good water, lodgepole pine all around. Sold out a couple year ago and come down here. You know something? . . . I can't even remember why."

"I guess Lando Beckett sold you The Store."

"You know Beckett, I 'low you ain't a stranger here."

"I been away a few years."

"You're a young man . . . young voice. What's your name, son?"

"Pike. Yuma Pike."

"I'm Enos Slaughter." He reached blindly out, and Yuma gripped his hand. Slaughter held his tightly. "Brother, I wish I could see your face."

If you could, Yuma thought, you'd wish twice as hard you couldn't. "Mr. Slaughter, you best stay still now." He rose to his feet, looking off west. The light had turned pumpkin-colored, shaping toward sunset.

Standing, resting his spread fingers lightly on his hips, he had a curious indolent dignity. About average height, he seemed somehow smaller, probably because he was slimly built, a loose-strung bundle of wire and whipcord. But his chest and shoulders were broadly solid, bunched with smooth ropy muscles that were not heavy. His curly chestnut hair was cropped close to the hard angular shape of his head.

Nothing soft in his face either: it was the color of a coffee bean, squarish, chiseled to hard angles, with the sharp high cheekbones and arching hawk nose of his Apache father. Only his hair and the blue-green eyes that jabbed like turquoise arrowheads showed his white half; yet the Virginia lady who had mothered him had eyes darker than his, and hair that had been blond and straight. "You have hair and eyes like your grandfather," she had told him. "Like my father." That was a funny thing, too. Indian blood nearly always eclipsed white man's hair and eyes in one generation . . . not to say two.

After throwing the gear off his horse, he hobbled the animal on a patch of galleta grass by the willows. Then he gathered mesquite brush, built a tiny smokeless fire and cooked up a little grub. He was used to packing light; he carried only a few pounds of hard staple food and only a pint of water. His Apache boyhood had taught him to go for days on a few swallows of water. Food was always available if a man knew what it was and where to find it. Tonight, plenty of water close by, he allowed himself a luxury: coffee that was mesquite beans boiled with an ounce or two of Arbuckle's.

Slaughter wasn't hungry, but he asked again and again for water. He was still conscious, but that was all. His eyes and sunboiled skin were giving him considerable pain, but there wasn't much to be done about either. I guess I wait him out, Yuma thought. He thought also of Cipriano, feeling impatient now, but he couldn't just leave the man like this.

"Mr. Slaughter, you feel up to talking a little?"

"Sure, son."

Yuma rose from the fire and came over to squat down by him. "You know Cipriano?"

"Know about him."

"Wouldn't know his face?"

"Well, there was always Apaches come to The Store to trade. But if he was one, I never knew it."

"Those four Cherry-cows . . . I thought he might of been one."

Slaughter moved his head side to side.

"Never saw any of them before. They was real old-time broncos, all the trimmings. Breechcloths and tall moccasins and paint. But Cipriano, now. Last I heard, he was rounded up and put on reservation with his old man, Cuchillo, up at San Lazaro."

"He busted out a few days back."

"I guess young bloods. Those four siwashes was young."

Yuma bent his head, staring at the ground between his feet. "They got into the tulapai. Drinking and bragging. Then they rode over to the Agency House. When Sandy Campbell come out on the porch, they shot him dead."

"Christ," Slaughter whispered. "Sandy . . . I knew him. He had a wife and two girls. . . ."

"It was the usual thing. They left the bodies inside and set fire to the house. One of the Cherry-cow women had overheard Cipriano and the others talking it up. She told the Apache police, but time they got to Campbell's, Cipriano was gone."

"Lord, Lord," Slaughter husked. "The Army. Ain't the Army out?"

"Some troops from Fort Beaudry took the trail. But Cipriano is way ahead and moving fast. Mostly south, but he is jumping all over."

"Christ. We didn't hear a word."

"It's all happened too fast. Cipriano's been sending out little bunches in fours and fives, and they're hitting everywhere."

"Brother, you know a pretty sight about it all."

A smile he didn't feel stretched the muscles of Yuma's jaws. "I just come from Fort Beaudry," he said. Afterward wondering why he'd lied. What did it matter?

"You been up north then."

"Been all over."

To cut off more questions, Yuma rose and walked around the mud shed. He put his shoulder against a corner and lighted one of his Spanish cigars, relishing the stinking, eye-stinging fumes. He stared off west at the gold and old-rose of sunset, feeling the heat drain out of the ground as the cooling air soaked it up. To the north rolled the bald crowns of the Santa Catalinas; southward lay the purple serrations of the Santa Ritas. Bending east and south into Mexico was the San Ignacio range.

Cipriano was working down toward the Ignacios. Cutting a bloody lightning-quick hundred-mile swath by diffusing his force of hotbloods into small parties that gave the Army nothing concerted to tail. Hitting the hamlets and ranches inside that hundred-mile cut before the inhabitants could be alerted to danger. Apaches never traveled in large bunches; they lived off the country; there was never enough food or water for many. Nine out of ten war parties numbered from ten to thirty warriors; Cipriano's old band had never ranged above fifty, and his present bunch, at a rough guess, contained twenty men or less.

It was an old tactic of Cipriano's — splitting his band into bunches of fours and fives and scattering them. Hitting by surprise, fewer than a half-dozen Apaches could take groups of whites twice their size. They could rape, murder, plunder, burn, and be far away within the hour. Or if they did bite off too much, they could pull out and vanish, ghostlike, in seconds. The band might split up and rendezvous this way many times before it reached the border. By that time it would have spread a disproportionate lot of havoc and fear over hundreds of square miles, with the probable loss, at most, of two or three men.

Yuma had gotten lucky, tracking south from San Lazaro. He'd quickly cut Cipriano's trail. But his luck had run out just as quickly after finding where the war chief had divided his party. Having no idea which bunch was led by Cipriano, all he could do was choose one group and follow it. Three times in the past two days he'd come upon the carnage the four Chiricahuas had left in their wake. First, two middays ago, an emigrant wagon, the man and his wife butchered. Next morning, the body of a prospector, his own pick driven through his chest, his mules shot and strips of meat hacked from the carcasses. Late yesterday, a burned ranch house but no sign of the bodies. Doubtless they were under the smoking rubble.

The country was hell for tracking. The four had stayed ahead of Yuma, even gained on him a little. He might as well, he thought dourly, be saddled with a troop of soldier boys. At first, in fact, he'd fleetingly considered offering his services to the Army. The hell with that, though. One time had been enough.

It was two years ago this summer that he'd helped General R. B. Wheeler's troops corner Cipriano in the Dragoons. That was after Cipriano had gone out of his way to massacre a family of Mexicans he knew to be friends of Yuma's. In retaliation, Yuma had volunteered to guide Wheeler. Trapping the Chiricahua leader in his own stronghold had been a feather in the general's cap; he'd offered Yuma triple wages to be his Chief of

Scouts. He had argued, wheedled, pleaded; when Yuma had refused even to give a reason why not — or his reason for making an exception in this one case — the famed Wheeler temper had short-fused.

Cipriano.

Cipriano was his reason. He'd never have sided U. S. troops against any other Apache.

As far back as memory went, deep into childhood, rivalry had rubbed between them like a naked knife. Maybe it had been natural, as such things went. But a day had come when rivalry had exploded into hatred.

They had both turned thirteen that spring, he and Cipriano. Cuchillo's band had been camped by the headwaters of the Gila. Fresh meat was needed, and the timbered canyons above the Gila were filled with big and small game. The two boys, armed with bows and buckskin quivers of arrows, had gone out to try their luck. He, Yuma, was Gian-nah-tah in those days. And Cipriano had not yet won the Spanish war-name that he, like all Apaches so honored by the Mexicans, wore with pride. Then, he was still Tloh-ka, eldest son of Cuchillo, living in his father's shadow and filled with raw stirrings of ambition. The two boys often hunted together, but not out of comradeship. Only in the simple hope of outdoing one another.

They'd climbed like young goats up to a rocky spur. Tloh-ka led the way. He was older and bigger; his longer arms and legs gave him all the advantage. Yuma had kept up with him, he never knew how, and when they stood on the spur looking at the Chiricahua camp far below, Tloh-ka laughed.

"It has only begun," he said. "We have a lot farther to go. Maybe the *pin-da lik-o-yee* should run home to his pale mother."

"Do not call me a white-eyes again." The younger boy was grunting with exhaustion.

Tloh-ka, big and barrel-chested like his father, with the square primitive face of his Yaqui mother, laughed again. "You're right; *Ka-chu* suits you better. You'd make a good rabbit. Come on, rabbit."

They plunged into a shadowed canyon, climbing steadily. The smell of cedars was warm and resinous where sunlight tangled in their deep-down branches. Coming out on the canyon rim, they followed a narrow trail along the rimrock. It was quite suddenly, while rounding a shoulder, that they found themselves facing *shoz-di-ji-ji,* the black bear.

She was an old bear, her muzzle silver-shot, and she had whelped this spring. Even irritable and ugly-tempered, she should have turned tail. But she didn't. Maybe her cubs were too close by. Maybe it was only the cramped trail: no way to retreat but backward. Anyway she stood fast, growling.

Tloh-ka, in the lead, hissed: "Now be quiet, *Ka-chu!*" And fitted an arrow to his mesquite bow.

The bear roared as the sharp quartz head ripped into her shoulder. She rushed and reared. Tloh-ka yelled as he and the bear plunged together off the ledge. They didn't fall far, maybe fifty feet, rolling down the sloping canyon wall into the cedars.

"Gian-nah-tah!" Tloh-ka screamed.

He had fallen between a couple of cedar boles and was wedged there. He was bleeding from lacerations by claws and rocks, his leg bent under him at an impossible angle. A few yards away, the bear climbed to her feet and shook herself. She sniffed the ground, then turned her head. Tloh-kah screamed again.

Gian-nah-tah shouted at *shoz-di-ji-ji* and heaved a rough-edged chuck of rock. It hit the bear's wounded shoulder. Raging, spittle streaking her jaw, she swung her head around and up. Scrambling and hooking in her claws, she came lumbering up the steep canyon side. He sank an arrow into her neck. A second went still deeper. The third, just as the bear fixed claws in the rimrock to drag herself up, was shot into her ribs behind the right foreleg. She slid back to the bottom in a miniature avalanche. . . .

Yuma had a bearskin robe and a beautiful claw necklace; Tloh-ka had a broken leg, a subsequent limp that didn't go away for years, and claw marks that he would carry to his grave. Scars of disgrace, brands of ineptness and fear that would never fade from his body or his memory. Yuma never mentioned the details that would have reflected on Cipriano, but it didn't matter that nobody else knew. Cipriano knew. And so did Yuma. To the war chief, that meant undying hate for the one who'd saved his life.

This time Yuma wasn't bothering with the Army. All they'd do was track Cipriano down and again return him to San Lazaro. Which wouldn't settle a thing.

He walked back to the fire and threw on a few sticks.

"Pike."

Slaughter's voice was very faint, hardly reaching him. Yuma went over and hunkered down by him again. Slaughter raised one hand and held it palm out toward the horizon.

"That's the sunset, ain't it? Over there."

"That's right."

"I can feel it yet. Warm. But she's going fast, that old sun, dusk soon. Pike."

"I'm listening."

"Loan me your gun."

Yuma said nothing.

"You got a handgun, ain't you?"

"I got one."

"Then shove it in my hand and walk away." Again Yuma didn't answer. Slaughter whispered: "Christ, boy. It ain't all this hole in my gut. I near roasted alive all day. You know how I look — I know how I feel. Won't get a wink of sleep tonight. Can't wear clothes on this skin . . . can't even abide the touch of a blanket on me. Can't lay next a fire. You want me to last out the night like this?"

Yuma looked at him. How much longer did he really have? And what the hell could a man say?

"There's another thing. I give ear to how you move about. Quiet, like an Indian. Listen. Maybe it won't do no good, maybe I'm wrong to ask. Could be too late. Likely is. But there's my girl . . . there's Beth Ann. She was alive when they took her away." His voice was a reedy twitch of sound. "Oh Jesus. Jesus, Pike. She was only eighteen."

24

"You asking me to go after 'em?"

"A man moves like you . . . he might be able to . . . something."

"All right. I'll do my best."

"God bless you." Tears spilled from his opaque eyes. "Listen, Pike. I give ear when they rode off, they headed southeast, I'd swear."

"I'll pick up the trail first light."

Yuma started to rise, but Slaughter's hand shot out and hit his arm, then closed fingers over it. "Pike, your gun. Come on, boy. Don't leave a man like this."

"I don't aim to leave you."

"You got to . . . first light. For her sake, you got to find them soon. And I don't hanker to spend the night this way."

Yuma pulled the hand away. Jerking out his Colt, he cradled the butt in Slaughter's palm.

"Thank you. Thank you, boy."

Yuma got up and walked swiftly away. Beyond the willows, he stopped. Twilight was pooling on the river. Coolness rose off the bank and water, but he was sweating. Had he done right? He didn't know. All he knew was that it was a sorry thing to have to do.

One bullet for Slaughter. And one for Cipriano. The thing would balance out then.

If he hadn't saved Cipriano that day above the Gila fifteen years ago. To get thinking that way was wrong, it was unreasonable. But the fact remained. Cipriano had a quality. Victorio, Tana, Juh, Geronimo — all the great war chiefs had it. If Tloh-ka had died, Cipriano's massacres would never have been.

The goddam ghosts. Scores of them. If he didn't exactly live with them, still they'd soured the back end of Yuma's thoughts too long. Time the swollen list was cut short. He knew the twisted brain that lived in Cipriano's head, knew it as he did his own hand. He could find Cipriano where no one else could; he could cancel an ancient debt with one bullet.

A bullet for Cipriano.

Off behind him the shot came. Echoes slammed against the ridges and washed back into stillness.

CHAPTER TWO

Yuma lay on his belly at the edge of the mesquite and trained his fieldglasses on the camp. The four Apaches were resting on the ground, talking, chewing strips of jerky, gesturing considerably as they talked. He swept their faces carefully with the glasses.

He knew one of the Chiricahuas. Sus-to, a boyhood friend. The others were strangers, therefore not members of Cuchillo's old band.

That wasn't strange. Cuchillo had given up the fight long ago. The old guerrilla leader, fiercest of all the war chiefs, had come to see his fight as hopeless. Privately, he might applaud his half-Yaqui son's intransigence; publicly, to keep on the good side of his white captors, he had forbidden his young men to ride with Cipriano.

It wasn't that simple, of course. An Apache warrior was his own man. Only on a war party did he give a temporary and grudging allegiance to a leader, a war chief. But even tired and old, frequently sick or stuporous from the illegal whiskey given him by his friends among the white officers at Fort Beaudry, Cuchillo still commanded enough respect and influence to be heard and obeyed. Cipriano had been forced to recruit most of his following from other bands.

Yuma moved the glasses to the girl. She was doing all the work, of course. Limping as she moved about, picking up sticks of wood here and there. She returned to the fire with a small armful of sticks and dropped them on the blaze.

One of the Apaches leaped to his feet and

stalked over to her. He scattered the twigs with his foot and gave her a hard cuff. After a half-minute lesson on how to feed sticks into the fire gradually, keeping it compact and smokeless, he gave her another cuff. They laughed a little, watching her gather up the scattered sticks, then plunged back into intense discussion.

Yuma wouldn't have given a cold beer to learn what they were saying. He could guess.

It had been easy to track them after he'd left Slaughter's place this morning. The trail had covered stretches of fawn-colored waste dotted with ironwood and mesquite thickets, palo verde and catclaw. To the white man, at least, it was all waste. Not to the Apache, who could go waterless as long as any coyote or chaparral cock. And not to Yuma. Also the quartet had loafed along with their prisoner, keeping on a rough line east by southeast through the day. Apparently they were bored, or just surfeited, with the easy pickings they'd so far found. They had made a midday camp to relax and talk things over, and it was here that Yuma had found them.

The two younger men seemed to be mildly arguing with Sus-to and the other warrior. Should they go on to rendezvous with Cipriano and the others, or should they hunt for more easy white-eyes prey? That, Yuma guessed, was the gist of the debate.

Until Slaughter's, he'd had no intention of quickly overhauling the four. They held no interest for him beyond his knowing that if he stayed with them, they'd lead him to rendezvous with the main party and Cipriano. Such track as he'd already found had made him reasonably sure that Cipriano himself wasn't among these four. He hadn't overtaken them merely to confirm a near-certainty.

His reason was the girl. Not that he felt a particular sensitivity about Beth Ann Slaughter's fate; he'd admit to a more personal concern if she were Mexican or Indian. He had no brief for rape or rape-killings, that was all, no matter who committed them. That included gangs of white militia who had made games of burning down Indian villages, shooting anyone who got in their way, and carrying the women and girls off in the brush. If the victims ever turned up, it was like as not with a bullet in the brain. That sort of thing happened a lot, but you never heard mention of it from the same white-eyed mealy-mouths who yawped about violations against the sanctity of white womanhood.

The Slaughter girl was bruised and limping from a beating or two, but she looked all right otherwise. Or more accurately, she didn't appear to have suffered any more physical damage — at least any of a different sort — than had been done her in the first place.

The thing was, they might kill her at a moment's whim, just as whim had spared her life so far. A good reason for not delaying the fulfillment of his promise to the dying Slaughter. He had to try to get the girl out alive, even if it meant giving up his plan of following the four Chiricahuas to Cipriano.

Shifting like a snake, Yuma wormed on his stomach back into the brush. When he was off skyline, he rose and catfooted down the long ridge, then circled back to where he'd left his zebra dun. The sun was low, its flat rays sheeting the rocks with pine fire. He had first spotted the Apaches from a ridge across the valley. Though he'd been a lot nearer to their camp on that side, he had worked patiently around to a far ridge to put the sun at his back and to study the camp without risking sunflash against the glasses.

For what he planned next, though, the closer in he could get, the better.

He'd considered other ways and had

discarded all of them. If they were whites, he could wait till night, create a diversion, maybe run off their ponies, then steal the girl out of camp. He could manage it without killing and with a minimum risk to the girl. But trying the same thing on Apaches would be suicidal.

Maybe what he'd decided on wasn't a whole lot better. It would at once cut the odds to three. Maybe even to two, if he were lucky. But this way, killing couldn't be avoided. Neither could the fact that odds would still be against him. It was also possible that the Chiricahuas, finding themselves attacked, would kill the girl at once.

He changed his boots for the curl-toed moccasins he carried on his saddle. Slipping his Sharps from his saddle scabbard, he checked the load: four lethal inches of brass and lead. He knew what it could do, this old buffalo gun. That was why he had borrowed it for this mission and the shot he hoped to get at Cipriano. It would double the killing chances of any man average with a rifle. It would hammer flesh and bone to a pulp; it would rip up internal organs like wet paper.

He quickly scaled the shallow ridge; getting over the top unseen was the ticklish part. He managed it by slithering between and around the plentiful clutter of boulders and brush mottes, keeping every obstruction available between himself and the camp below. It was slow going and the rocks were hot as hell. Once he was down off the slope, it was easier. The valley floor was broken, laced with gigantic rubble, dense with mesquite that clung in pale green clouds to the open patches.

He worked in as near to the camp as he dared, up to the base of two big rocks that he had marked with his eyes earlier. The rocks were wedged almost together. Hat off, he raised himself by inches till he could sight down the notch between them. He sized the whole thing at once: the horses off to one side, four Indian ponies and one of the swing team horses from Slaughter's station. The other Slaughter horses had been run off, this one kept for the girl.

Would they go for their mounts as soon as shooting began? Maybe, but a mounted man was a target. The camp was rimmed by more of the tall brush that had covered Yuma's approach; it would also shelter the Apaches, once they were alerted.

Sus-to and one of the younger men were on their feet now, striding back and forth as they argued, sometimes wheeling to face each other. The rest watched them. The girl was bent over the fire, feeding it sticks.

Yuma brought the Sharps level. Its octagonal barrel, dulled by a rubbing of vegetable matter, was almost the color of the rocks he was aiming between. For a moment he let the sights rest on Sus-to, hesitated, then shifted to the bigger Apache. He had just swung about, his broad coppery chest hanging steady in the sights.

The old rifle boomed mellowly. He'd never sighted in the borrowed weapon; the shot went inches high.

The .50 caliber slug almost tore away the Apache's lower jaw. He went over as if kicked by a mule, blood spraying from his shattered head.

Echoes sprang from the rocks; the ponies shuffled. The other warriors, as Apaches taken by surprise usually did, simply froze. Their training was directed toward one goal: never let an enemy take you off guard. Yuma had — so unexpectedly as to paralyze them for a long moment.

He nearly had a fresh cartridge breeched before the three moved; then it was like trying to tag brown lightning.

One Apache dived for his rifle, got it and rolled once as he hit the ground, then melted into the brush. Another sprang for his pony; its horsehair rein was loosely at-

tached to a branch. He freed it with a yank
and vaulted to the pony's back. On his feet
now, Yuma pulled down on the warrior as
he lunged his animal into the brush, but it
was already too late; the foliage swallowed
him. Yuma hastily swung his aim on Sus-to,
who had whipped out his knife and was
leaping toward the girl.

Yuma fired, this time overcompensating,
pulling his aim too low. The bullet snapped
Sus-to's ankle like a rotten stick. He plunged
down, landing on the fire. Howling, he
rolled wildly away from mold of ashes and
smoke. Then he floundered on his hands
and one knee toward the brush, his broken
leg dragging. Yuma let him go.

The girl stood as she was, hands full of
sticks, staring at the faintly writhing body of
the first Apache. She let the sticks drop and
sank to her knees, still staring. Just stay that
way, Yuma thought, thumbing in a fresh
load.

He sank back flat to the ground, listening
to the silence. He guessed that the two
Apaches who remained, one horseback and
one afoot, would swing around and converge
on the source of the shot. They couldn't
know who their enemy was, or his numbers,
but two wide-spaced shots would indicate
one man. Yes . . . they'd swing back.

Cradling the rifle in his bent arms and digging in his elbows, Yuma glided away belly flat through the brush to his right. It would be all stealth and stalk now, a stalk to the death; at least he wouldn't be a stationary target.

He squirmed along for a hundred feet under the lacy green canopy of mesquite. A stretch of sand and rock and a few tangles of catclaw gaped nakedly ahead. He reached its edge and waited. Splintery light rocked against his eyes. There was no noise out there, no hint of movement.

Take the chance, he thought. Draw some lightning. He scrambled up and ran low and fast for a cluster of rocks yards away. Suddenly a rifle opened up off to his left. He dived to the ground, hit it rolling, lost his rifle when his knuckles smacked on a sharp rock, and kept rolling. When he stopped face-down, two near ricochets screamed off the flinty earth; another flung pebbles against his leg. He scrambled one more yard and reached the clustered rocks and fell behind them.

His .45 gouged the trough of his hip where it pressed against a sun-hot stone. He shifted his body, eased the gun from its holster and waited. His luck the Apache was a rotten shot, but his rifle was gone and he was in an exposed position, pinned under the sun. And there were two of them. If two with rifles were to commandeer both sides of the clearing, he was a dead man.

Don't wait for it, he thought. Surging to his feet, he broke for the wall of mesquite on the clearing side away from the rifleman, running low to keep the rocks between them. Then brush crackled; hoofs drummed the ground.

Out of the tail of his eyes, still running, he saw the mounted Apache tear into sight and streak across the open, heels flailing against his pony's sides. He veered hard across Yuma's path, bearing down on him with a high taunting yip, a quartz-shod lance pointed.

Yuma snapped a shot at him, missed, then in mid-run flung himself out of the pony's way. He lit on his shoulder and hip, twisting over in the same motion, as the Apache thundered by stabbing viciously downward. His lance thrust scraped rock as Yuma completed his twist, falling on his back.

He pulled his pistol around in a tight arc, fanning every bullet in the gun at the Apache as he charged past. The warrior stiffened in a high contorted shape against the sun, his turning face dark and torn on the sun's hard brass-bright aureole. Loosely straddling his horse, he was dead and falling even before he was jolted completely free, and he pitched into the rocks like a shattered grainsack and sprawled brokenly.

Yuma lay where he was for a moment, listening to the pony crash away through the mesquite. Belatedly, remembering he was still exposed to the rifle-armed Apache, he flung himself sideways. He wouldn't make it, he thought, scrambling now for the shelter of brush. But he did; no shot came.

He reloaded his pistol and waited, heart pounding. Was the Apache out of shells? Had his rifle jammed? Whatever, the Apache warrior without a gun was still a deadly fighting machine.

Yuma edged to his feet, gun palmed; but stealth and quickness would be his best weapons. He passed through the mesquite, running, and into a forest of rock. He paused in a gravelly pocket, again, listening. Heat pressed like a dead hand; sweat streamed down his back and ribs. He waited for about a minute.

A lizard side-slipped from under a rock a few yards distant. It scratched sluggishly at the ground, raising thin puffs of dust. Suddenly it stopped and turned its head as if hearing something, then scurried under the rock again.

Yuma listened.

There. No more than the whisper of a moccasined foot.

He cocked his pistol, pressing it between his arm and side to muffle the noise. He placed the sound. *Now.* He moved up out of the pocket, toes curling hard against the sloping gravel. A pebble rattled unavoidably, then he was on solid rock and halting again.

No sound at all. The rocks were thick around him, splashed by dying sunlight. He moved through them, not quickly, and a prominent rock like an upended loaf caught his attention. It would hide all of a standing man's body; if he'd placed that noise right, it hid an enemy.

He kept on, loping on an almost string-straight line that would take him close past the rock. He went quickly, light-footed but not noiseless, making his steps deliberate, unhesitating, unsuspecting.

As he came past the tight-angled corner of the boulder, he pivoted away on his heel, his gun wheeling. The Apache was already in mid-lunge, bared knife flashing in his fist. Still in the motion of twisting aside, Yuma fired. The warrior, unable to stop his plunging body in its leap, was turned by the bullet. Somersaulting past Yuma, he smashed on his back.

He scrambled half up, facing around on his knees. Blood dyed the side of his calico shirt. He raised the knife and with his last strength, falling forward, drove the knife at Yuma's legs. Yuma moved his right foot sideways, the knife splashing into the ground between his feet.

Yuma sheathed his gun and settled on his heels, staring at the dead man. He wished there had been another way. Yet an Apache would understand; these had died as warriors would. The sun was still out, the hour of dying a good one; their souls would not wander in the dark that was eternal.

He took the Apache's knife and bandoleer of cartridges; he found the jammed rifle where the warrior had left it. He took that, recovered his own rifle and the other dead Apache's weapons, then tramped back toward the camp, feeling as if the earth were pulling energy out of his heels every step he took. Then he thought of Sus-to, and he hurried.

Coming in sight of the clearing, he halted, not quite believing what he saw. Sus-to, his face wrenched gaunt with agony, was dragging himself across the open ground toward the two rifles leaning against a rock. Beth Ann Slaughter was on her knees by the fire, exactly as he'd last seen her. She simply watched Sus-to inch his way along, flopping his way toward the guns, and did nothing at all.

The Apache was still a good six feet from the rifles when Yuma came loping into the clearing. Sus-to stopped, belly-down, his palms flat against the earth, his strained face turning. Seeing who it was, he showed no surprise. His eyes flickered darkly over the weapons Yuma carried.

He grinned. "*Ink-ta,* Gian-nah-tah."

Yuma scooped up the two rifles, carried all the weapons across the clearing and dumped them on the ground far out of Sus-to's reach. Then he moved across to the girl. He bent, a hand on her shoulder. "What's wrong? Miss?"

She didn't look up. He shook her gently. "Miss Slaughter."

She slowly raised her face, no trace of expression in it. Her eyes, he saw now, were wide and vaguely startled, a look that was stamped in them. He shook her again. "Beth Ann!" Her face and eyes were unresponsive, and she let her chin sink till her gaze touched her scratched hands. Christ, he thought. That's just fine.

"*Ya-ik-te,*" Sus-to said. "She is not present."

"Can you get on your pony?"

"I do not know."

"If I put you on it, can you ride?"

Sus-to shrugged, grinning. "Why would you do this?"

"So that you can tell Cipriano where you saw me."

Sus-to laughed, his eyes glinting hotly. "You are funny, *sheek-a-say.* The arrow, *kah,* could not come faster than Tloh-ka will come when I tell him I have seen you. Pah! Kill me now, Gian-nah-tah. It is a good joke, but it is ended."

Yuma shook his head. "There are enough dead."

"It was the woman — for her?"

"Yes."

"She is your woman?"

"No. Listen, *sheek-a-say.* It would not matter if you were all *pin-da lik-o-yee* and she were one of our *Be-don-ko-he* women, a Chiricahua. It would be the same. This you understand?"

"No. You are not one of us; that is all I understand. Not a *Shis-in-day,* not a *pin-da lik-o-yee.*" Sus-to spat. "You are like the bat, Gian-nah-tah; not quite mouse, not quite bird. I do not know what you are."

"There are enough dead," Yuma repeated. *"Tats-an."* He lifted the Apache up till he

41

could stand on his good leg, then supported him over to his pony and helped him mount.

"I think maybe it is this," Sus-to said then. "You looked for Cipriano, but you found us. The woman spoiled it, eh?"

Yuma passed him the horsehair rein and stepped back. "Go. Tell Cipriano what you will."

"En ju."

It was the non-committal Apache grunt that usually meant anything at all. Sus-to kneed his mount into motion and put him across the valley, heading north.

CHAPTER THREE

"Look," Yuma said, "what about family? You got any relatives any place at all? Is there a name . . . anything?"

She sat on the ground hugging her drawn-up knees and staring at the fire. She said nothing.

Yuma swore gently.

He had tried talking to her off and on for hours, and had gotten nowhere. She hadn't said a word since her rescue. She responded a little to the sound of his voice. She obeyed commands, simple orders to stand up, sit down, eat, or drink, but she went through the motions as unfeelingly as a machine. At first he'd thought she might have been hit on the head, but her scalp showed no cut or abrasion. She was bruised and scratched and dirty, but not really hurt that he could tell; even the limp seemed nothing more serious than a twisted ankle. It had to be all in the mind; what the hell he could do about that, he didn't know.

He chucked some more mesquite wands on the fire. The flamelight curled up against the concave sandstone walls looming overhead. He had made camp deep in this slender notch in a cliff some miles north of his encounter with the Apaches. The fire was hidden; the walls reflected the heat.

After turning the remaining Apache ponies free, he had stripped the moccasins from one dead warrior. These replaced the girl's shoes, which were falling apart. Then he'd examined the small arsenal of rifles, pistols, and knives he'd taken from the bodies and decided they were worth bringing along. They wouldn't add too much weight lashed together and slung from his saddle, and they'd bring a fair price from any gunsmith in the second hand market. Afterward he'd mounted Beth Slaughter on her swing team horse and, having made sure she could hold the saddle, had tied a lead rope from her rein to his pommel and had pointed his horse north, using what daylight remained to put the dead Apache behind him.

North lay the Haines & Harmer stage road. Maybe, with Cipriano's warriors ghosting across the territory, the line had suspended its runs; but maybe not, and it seemed his best bet. The girl needed a physician, a good one, and that meant getting her to one of the larger towns. Tubac or Silverton seemed likeliest, both were on the Haines & Harmer run, and both about an equal distance away — depending if you went east or west. If the stages were still running, one of them could get the Slaughter girl to that sawbones a sight faster than he could, held to a plodding gait on her account. She seemed to handle a horse all right, but in her dreamlike state he couldn't risk a faster pace.

With only a few hours of daylight left, they hadn't gone far before he'd chosen this night camp. The Haines & Harmer road was still a good thirty miles away. He gave the fact a good deal of thought.

North. Sus-to too had been heading north.

Sus-to probably didn't know exactly where Cipriano was now, but he'd have a fair idea. There were places the Apaches knew of, age-old council sites and camping places they'd return to again and again. All tribes had them; tribal people could home in on them like trained pigeons. Couple that spark of intuition with whatever loose agreement Cipriano's divided bunch had made as to a rendezvous, and Sus-to wouldn't be long finding them.

Once Cipriano knew that Sus-to had seen Yuma and where, the war chief would drop everything to take up his trail. Yuma was sure of it, and he didn't like it. The roles would be reversed; Cipriano would become the hunter, he the hunted. If Cipriano found him while he was still saddled with the girl, he wouldn't stand a chance in hell of getting either Beth Ann Slaughter or himself out alive.

Would Sus-to tell? Hard to say. A lot hinged on the Apache's whim. Even if a boyhood friendship no longer counted for anything, he had not spared Sus-to's three comrades. Predicting the Apache mind was like flipping a coin: it could turn up gratitude as easily as betrayal.

Well, not much he could do but keep his eyes open. One thing he knew: if not for the girl, he'd be free to head any way but north and minimize the chance of a confrontation with Cipriano. But her condition meant his choosing the way that would put her in a doctor's hands as quickly as possible.

He looked dourly at her across the fire. She was shivering in the calico rag that remained of her dress. What the hell, he thought, and got up to pile more wood on the blaze. Then he unrolled his Saltillo serape, a warm fabric so close-woven it would turn rain, and draped it around her shoulders. She pulled it tight around her and went on staring at the fire. Its heat seemed to rouse her some. She made the first move she'd made without being told to, raising a hand to touch the matted tangle of her hair. She tried to comb it out with her fingers, a slow, absent, half-caressing motion of combing. Yuma got a wooden comb out of his gear and held it out to her. She looked at it a blank moment, then took it.

She was kind of pretty, he supposed, if you liked them ordinarily pale (badly sun-burned now) and on the thin side. Her hair, rippling out in the firelight as she combed it, was honey-blond like his mother's had been, only darker. It made him think back to when he was a boy sitting by a stream, watching his mother wash and dry her hair and comb it out, a fall of pale-gold fire in the sunlight. He remembered being ashamed of her sometimes because she was not as other mothers; yet he had secretly thought her hair beautiful and had bloodied the faces of playmates who had mocked him and her with taunts of "White-eyes! White-eyes!"

He remembered his fourteenth summer well, because that was the summer that Cuchillo's band had finally been brought to bay by U.S. troops and taken to the reservation at San Lazaro. Until then, his boyhood years had been mostly spent in Mexico where Cuchillo had terrorized the Sonoran villages and the goods-laden *conductas* coming to and from Hermosillo. He'd never seen a white woman other than his mother except for two or three fair-skinned *grandee* ladies — and those in the ugliness of death and massacre. At San Lazaro there were two white women: Mrs. Campbell, wife of the Indian agent, and Mrs. Pike, wife of the Rev. Judah Pike, the missionary. Mrs. Campbell was young and pretty, Mrs. Pike middle-aged and ugly, and that was when he realized for the first time that there were two kinds of beauty, Indian and white, and that his mother had been beautiful.

Had been. Even then, by the time of Cuchillo's capture, there was nothing about Tes-al-bes-tin-ay, second wife of Cuchillo, to remind anyone of Rena Millay, the young Virginia belle. Her skin was coarsened, weathered dark as a saddle, her hair almost completely gray. She had been so long with the Apaches that she moved and spoke and thought like one. When the officers at Fort Beaudry had questioned her, she had told them — so that they would not send her back to her Virginia people — that she was part Indian, and they had been willing enough to believe it.

She had been at San Lazaro all these years, and it was there that Yuma, taking time out from his aimless driftings, had gone to see her just four days ago.

They had stood by her brush *jacale* and talked. She was gray and gaunt, but her eyes still sparkled like clean amber in her stern handsome face; he thought it strange how young her eyes always stayed. She told him of what had happened a few hours before he'd arrived: Cipriano's murder of the Indian agent and his break from San Lazaro at the head of twenty-odd hotbloods.

"Now that your brother has killed *Nan-tan* Campbell," she said, "who will the chiefs in Washington send to replace him? So many agents are bad. We were lucky to have Campbell. Now that he is gone, what white man will speak for the *Shis-in-day?*"

"It is not my business," Yuma said. "And do not call Cipriano my brother."

"You are both sons of Cuchillo."

"Let Cuchillo tell me I am his son."

"You know he will never do that."

He knew. He had heard the story many times.

Of how his mother's father, Col. Theron Millay, had been in command at Fort Spanning when news had reached the Arizona outpost that the South had seized Fort Sumter. With the war that he had hoped might be averted a sudden reality, the colonel decided to resign his U.S. Army commission and return East to fight for his native Virginia. The Apaches were out; both Mangus Colorado and Cochise were raising hell up and down the territory. But Colonel Millay refused either to delay his departure or to ask for an escort of federal troops from Captain Charles, to whom he'd relinquished his command. Bundling his wife and daughter into a wagon, he had set out for Price City, forty empty miles to the east. On the lonely road, the party was attacked, the colonel and his wife killed, and sixteen-year-old Rena carried off.

Why Cuchillo hadn't killed her too, Rena Millay was never sure. He thought her ugly and often told her so. She suspected that he found some mystical link between her light hair and his personal medicine. Still he'd never touched her except in the night. But his first wife, the Yaqui woman, jealously hating the white-eyed intruder, had beat Rena viciously and often until the white girl once took away her stick and returned the beating. Thereafter the Yaqui woman had nursed her hatred in silence till Rena's son was born. Seeing the baby as a rival to three-year-old Tloh-ka, her own son by Cuchillo, she'd set about to undermine the white woman and her son in Cuchillo's favor. Subtle, patient, untiring, she'd succeeded so well that finally Cuchillo had turned both Rena and her son out of his lodge.

Sour memories that ran strongly through Yuma's mind as he and his mother stood by her *jacale* and talked.

"Forget Cuchillo," she told him. "Think of the people. Because of your brother, the *pin-da lik-o-yee* will make us all suffer. Help the pony soldiers find him as you did before."

He considered it, then shook his head. "No. Not this time."

That was the moment he had decided that Cipriano must die by his hand.

Your brother. His mother had shrewdly probed a private nerve with those words. Always he tried not to think of the blood tie, but how could he separate it from the heavy responsibility he felt where Cipriano was concerned? The Yaqui woman was long dead, but the vicious seed she'd planted had flourished and grown. If Cipriano weren't his brother — half-brother — the squabble for their father's favor would never have been. Conversely, if not for the blood link, he probably wouldn't have saved Cipriano from the bear.

Yes. Tes-al-bes-tin-ay was right. *Your brother.* It was like a muddy spot in his eye, that link — confusing his thoughts even as it drove him to hunt Cipriano down.

Firelight ribboned between Yuma's half-shut eyelids as he thought his thoughts, arms crossed on his knees. He looked at the girl. She was still combing her hair long after the last snarl was out, passing the comb teeth through its length and smoothing it with her hand after each pass. He got up and tramped around the fire and held out his hand. She made a little protesting noise, hugging the comb to her.

"All right. You can keep it. But you got to sleep now."

She only stared at him, unmoving, hands clasped around the comb. "Sleep," he repeated. He got his bedroll and spread it out beside her, then took the serape and went back to his side of the fire. She lay down on the ground sheet and curled up on her side, pulling the blanket over her. She never took her eyes off his face. Yuma threw the serape around his shoulders and sat close to the fire. He was starting to doze when she spoke in a sudden shrinking voice:

"Who are you?"

She was still curled up, he saw, watching him. Her blank look was gone. He started to get to his feet.

"What you going to do?" she shrilled.

"Nothing."

"Don't you dast come near me!"

"All right."

Yuma sat back. He watched her roll to a sitting position, looking around her. "My God," she whispered. "Where am I? Who are you?"

"Name's Pike. I'm the man who saved you from the Indians."

"Indians?" Her hands flew to her mouth. "Pa? Where's my pa?"

"Your pa is dead."

"Dead." She stood up slowly, palms flattened against her face. "I don't believe . . . they didn't kill him."

"He was near dead when I found him. Before he went, he asked me to find you."

"No, that ain't true . . . he ain't dead.

You're lying to me."

Yuma got to his feet. "Listen now."

"Don't you dast touch me!"

"I ain't about to. But you got to listen."

"No!" Her eyes were black with panic. "My pa wouldn't a' sent you! You're a damn dirty siwash yourself!" She came around the fire toward him, crying, "You dirty lying Injun!" She hammered at his face with her fists. "Dirty siwash Injun!"

He caught her wrists and she began kicking. He slapped her. Almost full strength, but catching himself at the last moment. The slap knocked her away. She sank to the ground, sobbing, clawing her fingers at the sand.

"You don't need to worry about being touched," he said.

He picked up his serape and his rifle, along with the bundle of Apache guns — figuring he didn't want to leave a weapon in her reach — and walked to the mouth of the canyon some six yards away. He sat down in the narrow mouth, back braced against one wall, outstretched feet almost touching the other wall. He pulled the serape around his shoulders and laid his rifle across his lap. The other end of the canyon boxed off, and with him at the mouth this crazy girl wouldn't try to slip out in the night.

She lay in the sand awhile just watching him, crying a little. Then she got up and went back to her blankets. Maybe, he thought, a night's sleep would do her some good.

All night she tossed and moaned in her sleep, waking him several times. He didn't know what to expect from her come morning. But when he woke her in the gray hour of pre-dawn and gave her a few orders relative to breaking camp, she obeyed without argument. She was stony-quiet, her eyes murderous every time they turned on him. The fact that she'd snapped out of her mental paralysis or whatever it was didn't make him feel a jot easier. Something in her still wasn't ticking right.

The dawn was still new, a pink-pearl light serrated by the black broken lizard-spine of the San Ignacios, as they rode out. In an hour the sun was burning like an unwinking lemon eye against their right sides. The country was monotonous: gravelly stretches of bear grass and prickly pear, sand-colored open slopes with patches of brittlebush and cliffrose, a few mildly wooded places where piñon and scrub oak sank down tenacious roots.

Yuma worried about the water situation. He had taken none himself since yesterday and had carefully rationed the girl's intake to a swallow now and then. It had worked no hardship on him — not yet at least — but she'd need more water soon. An Apache might know the secret seeps or get along on the rancid liquid he carried in a piece of horse intestine with the ends tied off. But for whites, all travel in this part of Arizona was circumscribed by the few waterholes in hundreds of square miles, those widely scattered and undependable by midsummer. A traveler from the beaten paths had to plan his route to touch these waterholes or he was dead before he started.

The nearest water that Yuma knew of was at Jaramillo Wells roughly ten miles to the east, but he'd never heard of it staying wet in a dry season. The next closest was Redondo Tanks at a lava reservoir, or rather a series of them; it was usually reliable all year around but lay about thirty miles to the northwest. The Haines & Harmer road was many miles nearer. Best to continue due north to the road and gamble that a stage would be along soon.

Before noon, he saw a hazy yellowish plume lifting along the horizon. Another pair of eyes might have seen anything from a dust devil to a mirage: he knew it for what it was. Dust raised by a sizable body of riders. He didn't have to guess. Cipriano, he thought. And my old pal Sus-to, leading him straight to where we were.

He kneed his horse away at right angles, jerking the girl's mount along, his eyes on a bulgy lift of ridge. It wasn't over two hundred yards away, but he held them to a walk. Even a modest trot would raise enough dust to give them away to distant Apache eyes. The ridge was low, knobby with broken rock and covered with scraggly brittlebush. Scrub oak around the base would hide their horses from any but a close observer. He dismounted, told the girl to stay where she was, and catfooted up the ridge, field glasses in hand. He went up the last few feet on his hands and knees, and stopped at the ridge crown to train the glasses.

Belly to the ground, elbows bracing him partly upright, he watched for a long time. Finally he was sure that the horsemen were coming on a line that would sweep them past this ridge by many hundreds of yards. They were still too far away for him to pick out detail, but it was a dead-sure bet they were Cipriano's men. The only other sizable body of riders likely to be ranging abroad would be a cavalry troop, but any horse soldiers sent out so far wouldn't be close to Cipriano's whereabouts yet, certainly not this far south.

A scuffling noise below and to his back. He knew it was the girl; he looked back at her toiling up the slope. She stopped when his glance touched her. She had fashioned herself a kepi-like headcloth from odd strips of skirt and petticoat; it lapped over in front to shade her sunburned face.

"You want to come up," he said, "don't show yourself." Her eyes were uncomprehending and sullen, and he said: "Down on your hands and knees."

She did as she was told, moving awkwardly up beside him, keeping two feet away. She stared across the baking waste. The dust cloud was nearer; she saw it now.

"Why, that's — !"

She started to raise up; he choked off the movement and her words by driving her down hard with a palm flat between her shoulders.

"Apaches," he said.

She lay quiet under his hand, and he took it away.

A moment later he felt a jerk at his holster; she had yanked his Colt out, and she whirled away on her hip and side out of his reach, and scrambled to her feet. She stood a couple yards below him, the gun slanted up at him.

"They're Apaches," he said mildly.

"You're lying," she said between her teeth. "Those riders, they out looking for me. My pa sent them to look."

Yuma eased slowly off his belly and onto his heels, turning, till he crouched facing her. "Told you. Your pa's dead."

"You're lying!" She screamed it, her fingers white-knuckled.

"You got to cock it first."

He came off his haunches as he said it, moving down fast and snaking out a hand, clapping it around the gun-frame and pulling the gun away. She stumbled backward from him and fell down, scrambling up again several yards below him. Yuma moved a yard or so down to put himself off skyline, then halted, watching her patiently.

"I'll say it once more. Your pa is dead. Stone dead. I buried him."

"He's not, he's not, he's not!"

She was yawping hysterically, lunging at him, hands up and fingers curved to claw his face. Out of patience, he slapped her hard, twice. She backed off, her mouth dissolving in a scream. He had to smack her again, even harder, to shut her up. She dropped to her knees, wiping a palm across her split lip, then looked up, her eyes unfocused with blind staring hate.

"Dirty siwash scum," she whispered. "Stinking dirty Injun."

He watched her distorted face, thinking, I killed three men I never seen before on your account. For an instant that was all he could think, and a red violence thickened his brain. He took a tight grip on himself, then wheeled and tramped back to the ridgetop, crawled the last few yards and flattened down again.

The horsemen came on, going past the ridge more than a thousand yards off. Through the glasses, he was able to make out a good many details about the Apaches, how they were armed and what their numbers were. He counted twenty-one, meaning that all the small raiding parties had pulled back together. All but the one he had wiped out excepting Sus-to. And Sus-to was there, riding up by Cipriano.

Flanking the war chief on his other side was Cuchillo's brother, Es-ki-min-zin. He was easy to single out — lean, long, scarred, taller than most Apaches because of the Comanche blood he shared with Cuchillo on their mother's side. Yuma was surprised to see Es-ki-min-zin — whose voice had always counseled restraint, even in Cuchillo's heyday — riding with his firebrand nephew. Once it had been Es-ki-min-zin's influence with his older brother that had made Cuchillo realize the futility of continued resistance to the whites.

Yuma followed them with the glasses as they swung south and dropped out of range across a slow swell of land. Then he went down the ridge and told the girl to mount.

He didn't know how much time they had. Time enough, he hoped, to reach the road and then the sanctuary of a town. It depended on how soon the Apaches would cross their backtrail. If they went clear back to where Sus-to had last seen him, the edge would be one of many hours. If their route swung them across the tracks sooner, the margin could be cut a lot finer.

Cipriano could be sure Yuma wouldn't be waiting for him, but not which direction he'd go. North would be a reasonable guess, but Cipriano wouldn't gamble on a guess. It wasn't his way. He'd backtrack and hold the trail like a wolf.

A white pulse of heat simmered over the broken landscape; even Yuma felt its broiling oppression. A gritty ache leaked under his eyelids; his flesh felt sizzled. There were ways of coping with the midsummer desert, but they meant delays he couldn't afford.

He centered grimly on one goal: getting this miserable girl off his hands. Shed of that responsibility, he could pursue his mission of getting Cipriano his own way, on his own terms.

He looked back at her once, trailing him the length of her horse's leadrope. Her inflamed eyes reflected hate; her parched and cracked lips whispered it. And he didn't look back again.

CHAPTER FOUR

Dirty siwash. Stinking Injun. He wondered why that sort of vituperation still left him gut-shaken. It shouldn't any longer.

Last night the epithets had held no particular sting. Coming out of a nightmare and first of all seeing his half-Apache face was reason enough for her reaction. She was still incapable of fully accepting the situation, and that was understandable too. The blistering spittle of contempt she had spewed at him now was something else. The sort of thing her kind only partly bothered to hide when they were in their right minds.

White women. He knew about white women.

He thought of his fourteenth summer and the first white women he'd known. He'd never thought of his mother as white, only as a different sort of Apache. Young Mrs. Campbell, wife of the San Lazaro agent, had not liked Indians. She said they made her sick, and she kept a bottle of smelling salts in her reticule in case she had to go near them.

The missionary's wife was still another type. He used to hang about the mission and make himself useful in little ways, earning her notice. The Reverend and Mrs. Pike had finally commended his diligence by unofficially adopting him, even giving him their name. To get his three R's as taught by Mrs. Pike, he'd also swallowed her endless carpings on proper behavior, her tart homilies on the Good Life, and her birchings for the good of his savage soul. She was a good woman, but he'd wondered that her spine didn't snap under the weight of her granite-jawed rectitude. When, at sixteen, he'd left the reservation to feed his restless blood on hard knocks, it was with no regrets.

Shortly after, there had been Lana Belle, a big brassy woman with whom he'd spent several months in a remote, dirty roadhouse on the Nueces. The freshly widowed heir of its late proprietor, she'd kept him and fed him and taught him how to make sex more than a meal. He'd had reason to be grateful to Lana Belle, though he'd always figured she had plenty to be grateful for in return. Mostly warm and giving, she could turn on him with all the familiar epithets, drawling them with the peculiar loving meanness that only a Southern redneck could command. It would always leave him with the same shaken and gutted feeling, as if the manhood had been sucked out of him.

White women, sure. He knew about them.

At noon they topped a saddle between two ridges. Below was the stage road, a dusty ribbon snaking across the raw tan-red desolation. The terrain was humpy, the road winding quickly out of sight either way. Yuma knew just about where they were: almost halfway between Tubac and Silverton. A little nearer Tubac, but not by much.

Right now they needed rest. Here a rock pinnacle flung shade; it was as good a place as any. There was no fight left in Beth Ann Slaughter; she was almost falling out of her saddle. Her eyes were glazed, her body so stiff she could hardly move her arms and legs as he helped her to the ground. She slumped exhaustedly in the warm rock shadow, her throat working convulsively. Yuma gave her a handful of jerky and a couple of swallows of water, then had to wrestle the flask away from her. He shook it: not a half-pint left.

She wasn't in condition to go much farther; neither was her horse. Should they just stay in sight of the road and wait? What if the stage line had suspended its regular runs? You could wait for days. That being so, they might as well strike for Tubac at once. If a stage did happen along, nothing lost.

For Cipriano was on their trail, and Cipriano wouldn't wait.

Let the girl ride, he would walk. His rangy zebra dun was desert-bred; it needed little water and could live, when necessary, on tornillo beans and cactus with the spines burned away. He made the girl mount the dun, then trudged down the slope leading their horses. As soon as he saw the wheel tracks in the shallow dust of the road, he knew that a stage had passed only a few hours ago. The line had still been running as of this morning . . . but it might be the last stage for a long, long while.

Yuma swung toward the west and Tubac, tramping steadily. The broiling smash of midday heat caromed against his left side, but it didn't blunt his attention to details. He stopped suddenly and studied the ground. Unshod ponies had veered onto the road here, throwing up dirt in a run, obliterating the wheel ruts.

Apaches. They had gone after the stage.

Just ahead was a bulging escarpment where the road curved out of sight. Yuma went on slowly, nerves tightening — though he knew that whatever had happened to the stage and its people had happened hours ago. Coming around the bend, he saw what he had expected.

The stage was off the road, the dead horses sprawled in a bloody tangle of flesh and harness. But no dead people.

Yuma tramped over to the coach, going slow, looking for sign. There was plenty of it, enough to tell the story. As they always did, the Apaches had gone after the horses first. They must have hit a couple, causing the panicked team to run the stage off the road before more bullets halted them.

Yuma pulled open the coach door. Flies rose in an angry cloud. A man's body was stretched out face-up on the coach floor. Stone dead, the front of his shirt stiff with dried blood. His hands were folded neatly on his chest, his long legs doubled to fit in the coach's cramped width. He wore working clothes; his face below the whiteness of a hatline was weathered, arguing that he'd been the driver or the guard. A passenger — possibly, but driver and guard would be the first targets. Yuma turned the dead man's hands palms up. No ridges of callus such as a driver's hands, or those of other weather-burned men, always wore. This man was the guard.

As the Apaches wouldn't have taken them prisoners, the driver and passengers must have escaped. Only how? The sign said they'd been attacked by a large party, meaning Cipriano's whole bunch. The spent cartridge cases scattered inside and outside the coach said the whites had put up a fight. But the outcome, with the Apaches having plenty of rock cover all around, should have been inevitable. The paneled coach body was splintered with holes where the Apaches had poured in a withering fire.

The answer? Something had made the Chiricahuas pull off. It must have been Sus-to's arrival, after the shooting had drawn him to the spot. *I have seen Gian-nah-tah,* he would say. Those words would be enough for Cipriano. He wouldn't delay even for the minutes necessary to finish off some assured victims. He would order Sus-to to lead the way, and his men, though grumbling bitterly, would follow.

Yuma hunted around some more. He found signs to indicate that the whites had lost no time in clearing out after the

Apaches had left. They'd struck west for Tubac, all afoot. Sorting out their tracks, he found that two sets were made by men wearing flat-heeled boots. Of these, one pair would belong to the driver; the other might be those of a miner or a soldier — but not a cowman. Both of the other two men had been wearing "dancing slippers" — patent leather shoes. Finally, there were the small narrow prints of a woman's foot.

Five people. One a woman. None of them, likely, toughened for the kind of foot march they faced across miles of barren and sun-scorched country. Though proceeding on foot himself, Yuma guessed he wouldn't be long overtaking them; he only hoped they had water.

Within the hour, Beth Ann Slaughter began to slip from the saddle. He stopped long enough to lash her wrists to the pommel and her ankles together by passing the rope under the zebra dun's belly. The sun floated on a quicksilver dance of heat waves close to the horizon. Yuma's brain throbbed; heat particles prickled his half-lidded eyes. Cipriano or no Cipriano, they'd have to make a long stop soon. And find water, even if they had to lose precious hours by detouring far off the route to reach it.

For now, though, he clung to the road

because the tracks told him the stage people weren't far ahead. The woman and one of the dancing slipper boys were beginning to falter. The road bent around more masses of monolithic stone painted a flaming orange by the dropping sun.

"Stand there, son. Keep your hands clear, understand?"

Yuma promptly halted, unsurprised. The man's voice had come from just ahead and to one side, hollow and warning among the brush-tangled rocks. He'd probably thought that the brush hid him, but Yuma had already picked out the dark line of the rifle barrel, a man's slouch hat, hues of skin and clothing through the screening brush.

"I hear you."

"Stand like you are," the man said, then spoke over his shoulder. "All right, folks, come on out."

He moved then, coming into full sight, climbing down among the rocks till he stood in the road about a half-dozen yards from Yuma. A stocky weather-blackened gnome of a man, he had the dour, squinty, crushed-looking face of a bulldog. His rifle wavered carelessly off target, but he carried it like an extra arm and Yuma didn't doubt he could use it like one.

"What's your name, boy?"

Yuma stood easy, hipshot. "That your stage a couple miles back?"

"I'm the driver. Name's Crim Purdy." The man spat tobacco juice sideways. "Fair exchange?"

"Yuma Pike."

The others were coming through the rocks toward the road. They had been resting offside in a solid ring of boulders which offered shade as well as concealment. One man was in Army uniform; the other two were dressed as gentlemen. One was a Negro, which Yuma thought a curiosity. He had seen plenty of colored men, but none all duded up. The white fancy-dresser held back beside the woman, assisting her across the rocky ground.

The driver moved forward, rifle cradled on one arm. "That your wife behind you, son?"

"No."

"Good God Almighty." The driver stopped in his tracks, squinting. "What you got her trussed up like that for?"

"Only way to keep her on."

"That bad, eh?" Purdy spoke mildly, but his rifle was centered on Yuma's chest now. "I hope that's so, son. Maybe you better cut her loose now."

Beth Ann Slaughter was bowed forward in

a loose slump, only the ropes holding her partly upright. She raised her head as the driver spoke, looking blindly around her, then at him, disbelievingly.

"Mr. Purdy . . . oh, Mr. Purdy, is that you?"

"Christ save us! It's Enos Slaughter's girl." The driver swung hard on Yuma. "You got a story for this, brother, you better tell her sweet."

"I'll tell it. First we need water and rest."

He walked back to untie the girl. As he reached for the ropes on her wrists, she began to scream. "Mr. Purdy! God's sake, don't let him touch me!"

"That's enough, mister." The driver levered his Winchester. "Stand away from her."

"He's one of them," she babbled. "Can't you see that? Look at him!"

"Sure as hell," the man in uniform said softly.

He came forward till he faced Yuma from a yard away. He was broad as a hogshead with a thick ruddy face whose frame of curly black hair and beard made you think of a sulky buffalo. His pale blue trousers bore yellow cavalry stripes down the outseams; his rugged and faded blouse had darker patches on the sleeves where chevrons had been. The left sleeve was empty, rolled up and pinned below his shoulder stump. Disabled and discharged, Yuma thought.

"Look at this brown bugger's face. He's Injun, least half anyways, or my name ain't T. L. 'Sarge' Mulrooney."

"I'll watch him," Purdy said. "Cut the girl loose, Sarge."

The ex-soldier moved over to the zebra dun who sidled sideways, swinging his head around with a snap of his teeth. "Whoa, you randy devil!" Sarge dropped his hand to his holster flap.

"Ho-shuh," Yuma said quietly. The dun became motionless, his ears laid back.

"Go ahead," Yuma said.

Sarge took out a pocket knife, opened the blade one-handed and freed the girl, then helped her to the ground. She couldn't stand, and Purdy cursed when he saw her lacerated wrists. "Here, set her down in the shade. Someone fetch the canteen."

"John, bring it."

"Yes, Mr. Severn."

The white fancy-dresser had given the order; the Negro responded. He climbed back into the rocks, returning in a few moments with a canteen.

"Give it to Mr. Mulrooney," Severn said.

"Yes, sir."

Severn leaned lightly on a walking stick, looking politely bored, as if the whole business were an inexcusable annoyance. Slim, dapper, suave-faced, he had the soft and cultured accent of Old South gentry. His hair was pale as flax, his mustache neat, his Vandyke trimmed to a narrow spike. The whiteness of his linen suit was dust-filmed, the coat open to show a flowered waistcoat and a snugly holstered pistol. Both leather and pistol grip were worn; they had seen use. Judging Mr. Severn too quickly might be the biggest mistake a man could make.

Sarge let the girl drink, said, "More later, missy," and capped the canteen. He straightened up, grinning an ugly grin at Yuma. "Give me the loan of your rifle, Mr. Purdy. I aim to feed it down this fine bird's gullet, butt first."

"Not till we get the straight of this." Purdy nodded at the girl. "Now, Beth Ann, can you tell us what happened?"

"Him," she whispered. She lay in the shadow of a varnished flat-sided rock, her back propped against it. She rolled her head from side to side, raising a finger and pointing at Yuma. "Him, him, him, he done it!"

"Done what? Try to make sense, girl."

"She's half out of her head, Crim. Can't you see she is?"

The fourth passenger had spoken. The woman. She was tall and strong-boned, cool and regal and handsome. Her hair was flame-red and she was maybe thirty. She wore an expensive dress of dark watered silk. Dust had dulled its shimmery texture; she looked drawn and tired. Her skin was like rich cream, her chin and throat sun-flushed below the shadow of a wide-brimmed straw hat.

"I reckon she is, Duchess," Purdy said. "But we got to get the straight of things."

"Why not try him?"

She nodded at Yuma. She was, he thought, a hell of an impressive woman, almost queenly; except that her green eyes, crinkled at the corners from much laughter, held a certain bawdy wisdom, and her generous mouth was as sensuous as it was humorous.

Sarge snorted. "Hell, Duchess, that siwash will lie his head off."

"How do you know he will?"

"That ugly buck face of his says so. Likely one o' Cipriano's gang."

She smiled. "With that hair? Those eyes? Look at his clothes and gear . . . and his English, what little I've heard, is no worse than yours."

"That word — 'ho-shuh'," Purdy said. That's a word I heard Injuns use to calm spooky horses. Want to tell us you ain't part Injun, brother?"

"I ain't had a lot of chance to, was I minded," Yuma said mildly. "My ma was white, I was raised Apache. It's happened."

"Happen there's been half-blood hostiles who dressed white and talked good English, too." Purdy motioned with his rifle. "Now you come along this road with Enos Slaughter's girl tied onto your horse. Maybe you got a ready-sounding story for that."

"Four of Cipriano's Cherry-cows hit Slaughter's four days ago. They staked him out in the sun and took the girl. Time I came along, he was near dead. Before he died, he told me what happened and asked would I try fetching his girl back. I followed 'em and got her back. That's all."

"Brother, it ain't by a country mile. There's things here don't tally plain. You're a breed."

"I said it."

"You went after four bronco Cherry-cows and risked your hide to save a white girl's?"

"Looks that way, don't it?"

"All right, say you did, you took her from four 'paches. Maybe you want us to believe you all by yourself killed the four of 'em?"

"Three. One got away."

"Christ," growled Sarge, "what did I tell you?"

"Which way is Slaughter's from here?" Yuma asked.

"East," said Purdy. "About thirty miles this side of Tubac. We was heading that way."

"I was too, you noticed."

Purdy nodded grimly. "That's why you got to say your piece instead of me busting you wide open. Want to tell us you was taking her back to her dead pa?"

"You don't make it easy, mister."

"Any reason I should?"

Yuma let his glance shift from Purdy to the others, reading their faces. The woman's eyes were lively, interested, reserving judgment. Sarge, hot-eyed and surly, had already decided. Severn looked bored to indifference; the Negro's veiled stare showed nothing at all. Looking back at the driver, meeting his squinty, and guarded gaze, Yuma thought that Purdy wanted to be fair. Only having four passengers to look after, he had to be careful. Yuma decided he'd better explain again, and this time it had better be good.

"I was taking her to Tubac," he said. "I caught up with the 'paches southeast of here. . . ."

He told what had happened in as much

detail as he figured was essential to convince them of the truth, particularly of how Beth Ann Slaughter had come to her present condition. All that he omitted telling was how he had freed Sus-to, saying only that one Apache had gotten away. Since the girl had been in shock, he didn't judge she could contradict him, at least not in specific terms. He was right. All she did was keep sobbing. "He lies, he lies, he lies," to everything he said, and Purdy was no longer listening to her.

Yuma finished. The driver rubbed his chin, nodding. "Seems to fit right enough."

"Man," Sarge growled, "you're crazy. You said it yourself, he wouldn't kill no three o' his kind to save no white woman."

"Sense or not, I don't see his sign cuts no other way." Tipping up his rifle barrel, Purdy let the weapon slide down between his horny palms till the butt hit the ground. "If he took the girl, he'd of done his worst and killed her. He wouldn't be on no stage road heading for a white man's town. His story fits."

Yuma said: "How you fixed for water?"

"We ain't got half enough for us," Sarge said. "We sure-hell ain't sharing with no breed."

Yuma didn't even glance at him; he

watched Purdy. The driver shook his head. "That's our only canteen. Ain't got enough to last us till Slaughter's station, even without you two. We're in a fix, mister. Won't be another stage along for days. The line called off its runs two days ago soon as word come that Cipriano was out and pushing down this way."

"What about this run? Was you making a special one or something?"

"Sort of." Purdy spat sideways across his arm. "Mr. Severn, there, wanted to get to Tubac heap bad. Come into the division manager's office at Silverton and plunked down a wad of bills a horse would choke on. It bought him a stage and team. And me for triple pay, along with Jim Ralls and his shotgun. Old Jim." Purdy shook his head slowly. "They got him clean off, shot him right off the seat."

Yuma squatted down in the dust and rested his elbows on his knees. "You're right you won't make it. In this heat, take a strong white man used to long tramps to make it far as Slaughter's, even if he was packing plenty water."

"Son, there ain't no choice but to try."

"There's a choice." Yuma drew a line on the ground with his finger. "That's the road . . . right here, just north by west of us, is Redondo Tanks. You know the Tanks?"

"I know about 'em. Catch basins, I hear. Could be empty this time year. Or so fouled a man couldn't drink of 'em."

"Always that chance, but the Redondos ain't often dried up or gone bad. I make them worth trying for."

"I dunno. We'd have to swing way north off the road. Will mean a sight longer walk to reach Tubac."

"Thing is, you'll *reach* it." Yuma sketched with his finger. "You got enough water to make it to the Tanks. You fill your canteen there and head for Tubac on a long curve, like this . . . and here, around halfway between the Tanks and Tubac, there's a seep I know of. You fill up again there and push on to Tubac."

Purdy settled down on his hunkers, squinting at the map. "I dunno. It's one hell of a walk. Not for a 'pache likely, maybe not for you. But us, like you said, even if we had plenty water. . . ."

"You travel by easy stages. You rest often as need be and you lay up in the worse heat of day."

"What about grub? All we got is a few sandwiches in a rucksack."

"You ain't too proud to eat 'pache style, I can show you how to make do."

The driver grimaced. "Yeah, I don't doubt you know how. Hope you know this country too. Me, I be lost trying to find them Tanks."

"I know the country."

"Christ, Mr. Purdy," Sarge said. "You ain't about to trust no Injun, are you?"

Purdy spat at a rock and watched the spittle sizzle down to a brown stain. "You better start figuring it's gonna take an Injun to get us off this hot lid of hell alive."

"Well, by God, it's our necks, and we oughta put it to a vote, that's what I say."

Mr. Severn sauntered forward, twirling his stick. "That sounds fair enough. I vote to do as this gentleman suggests. Quite a generous suggestion, it seemed to me."

"That's what I don't like," Sarge grunted. "This breed got no reason to step for us. What d'you say, Duchess?"

"I say he's got no reason not to . . . at least none we know of. You're entirely too suspicious, Sarge."

"That's three for, one against," Purdy said. "Reckon it's your ball, Pike."

Yuma stayed as he was, tipping his head at the Negro. "One more to hear from."

Severn raised his brows and smoothed his mustache with his finger. "John votes with me."

"Like to hear him say it."

79

"That nigger don't have no vote," Sarge grumbled.

"Don't matter he does or don't," Purdy observed. "She stands three to one. His say won't make no difference either way."

"He's got a say," Yuma said softly. "Or you can all squat here and fry."

The woman laughed. "Don't be so damned sensitive, friend. He has a life to gamble, hasn't he? I call that a vote. What's your opinion, mister — ?"

"Twill, ma'am." The Negro's face was like dark stone. "John Twill."

"It's John or it's Twill," Severn said gently. "No 'mister' in it, is there, John?"

"No, sir."

Yuma scooped up a handful of sand and sifted it through his fingers, not looking up. "*Mister* Twill," he murmured, "how do you vote?"

"As Mr. Severn does, sir."

"It's Pike or it's Mr. Pike." Yuma raised his head, locking eyes with Severn. "No 'sir' in it."

Severn smiled, a mere stretching of his lips. He bowed slightly, ironically. "It would seem we're in your hands, Mr. Pike."

CHAPTER FIVE

There were a good four hours of daylight left, and Yuma meant to use them. The sun was low and some of the heat was lifting; it was the time of desert day for traveling. The stage people were already beat-out from a little trek under a broiling sun, but they would be a heap more so before this journey was ended: they might as well start hardening out now. He put it to them just that bluntly.

Sarge had no luggage that wouldn't fit in his pocket; the Duchess carried only a small carpetbag; Purdy had his rifle and a grub knapsack. Yuma watched John Twill pick up two bulky portmanteaus. The Negro was a big, superbly built man in his late thirties; he was too muscular to look entirely comfortable in his fine suit of black broadcloth. Even so. . . .

"One of them things is about as much as a man can tote in this heat," Yuma observed.

Twill straightened, hefting both bags. "Thank you, Mr. Pike. I can manage."

"Not for very far you can't. I was you, I'd strip them bags lean as I can get 'em, then pack what I really need in just one. Better shuck off your coat while you're about it.

Sweat too much water too fast under a coat."

"Mr. Pike. . . ." Severn had strode up; he tapped Yuma's arm with his stick. "It's just possible you don't understand. *Mister* Twill is a manservant in my employ. In return for wages, he takes my orders. I have no intention of abandoning my belongings, and *Mister* Twill is following an order to convey them to any place of my choosing. Is that clear, Mr. Pike?"

"It's clear enough."

"Then let him do his job, won't you?"

Twill had set down the portmanteaus to remove his coat. Tucking it under his arm, he picked up the bags again. As he swung away to clump across the uneven ground, the back of his wet shirt tightened across his broad powerful shoulders. Yuma felt his flesh crawl, seeing how the raised ridges of crisscrossing scars stood out under the cloth. Whip scars.

Yuma tramped ahead of the others, leading the horses. He thought of telling Twill to tie the portmanteaus on the zebra dun, but decided the hell with it. If Twill were damnfool enough to accommodate himself to such white-man crap, let him. The swing-team horse was almost done in, the tough zebra dun plodding with his head down. He had stripped every excess pound of gear from both animals, and he wouldn't risk a rider on either till they reached water.

Ahead, the land opened up vast and empty. The waning light drew rosy tints on the ridges and the far peaks, blurring the shadows to patches of violet fog. It was cooling some, but the six people following Yuma Pike were too exhausted to notice it much. None were used to walking; only Purdy and Sarge had more than a brushing acquaintance with the baking fury of a midsummer desert. Sarge stayed beside Beth Ann Slaughter, half-carrying the stumbling girl. Severn stayed beside the Duchess, giving her a gallant hand across the worst stretches, but he wasn't in much better condition himself.

Purdy moved up beside Yuma, tramping in silence for a minute. Then he said: "Funny thing about them Cherry-cows that hit us. You seen how they shot the horses and had us pinned down by the stage. Then all of a sudden they pulled off and rode away."

"You make out why?"

"Nope. Couldn't find rhyme nor reason to it. Had us dead to rights and they pulled clean out. We waited awhile, figured it was a trap. But they never come back." Purdy hacked and spat. "We judged it was Cipriano's whole bunch."

"Likely."

"What worries me, could be they'll come back. What you think?"

Yuma shrugged. "No telling. Could be any number of reasons why they rode off. Maybe a bigger piece of business somewhere. If it gets concluded quick enough, I allow they'll be back. Knowing you was all on foot, they will figure you ain't got far away."

"Yeah," Purdy said. "Been thinking on that. Wish t'hell we could fancy up a way to cover our goddam tracks."

"That'll take care of itself, once we're on the lava."

"Lava?"

Yuma nodded, swinging his arm in a half-circle. "You'll see it in a little while. All lava country up ahead. Whole stretches you couldn't track a buffalo herd on except for droppings. We'll stick on that where we can."

Purdy grunted his relief. "That's a load off, son, I don't mind telling you."

"If you can keep the others going another hour, we can camp on the lava tonight."

"I'll talk to 'em."

Purdy dropped back again, and Yuma heard his low, persuasive voice telling them.

What none of them knew was that losing the track wouldn't make Cipriano give up the pursuit. Knowing his hated half-brother was with their party, Cipriano would press ahead and take his chances. Nor would he be going altogether blind: he'd know that the whites needed water soon. In this direction, that could mean only Redondo Tanks.

Maybe, Yuma reflected, the smart thing to do — on his account as well as theirs — was to leave the party now and strike off in some other way, any way. If Cipriano caught them along with him, none would have a chance. Besides which, they were a goddam encumbrance. He could move a lot faster and farther by himself. Alone, even if Cipriano overtook him, he might still fight his way free.

Hell of it was that, supposing his presence did mean danger for these people, they'd be as bad off without him. For discounting Cipriano, he could pull them through the desert. They might be more dead than alive when they came out, but the difference between death and survival could be hair-fine as you please — so long as you survived. Anyway you looked at it, they were better off than if he'd never happened along. If, in fact, Cipriano hadn't gone chasing off south because Sus-to had reported seeing him, they'd be dead now, all of them.

Besides there was always a possibility that they could elude Cipriano. Reach the Tanks ahead of him, get their water and clear out. Better yet if they could avoid the Tanks entirely, but he didn't dare take the chance. Water. They had to have water.

What really nagged him, he supposed, was a dim sense of responsibility he felt toward these people. A twist of circumstance had made them his charges, and he didn't like the feeling a damn bit. Because of his blood mixture and because he had friends among both races, he'd always steered clear of taking sides in the larger war between whites and Apaches.

What did he owe this bunch anyway? Not a damned thing.

They came to the first ragged signs of the lava country, and Yuma went more carefully. He knew the region first hand, but he'd last been over it many years ago. It wouldn't be too hard picking one's way across the smooth sand stretches between the violent upthrusts of basalt, but his intention was to choose a hardrock trail that wouldn't be too rugged or too obvious. One that would hide their passage, yet let them move briskly along.

A gaunt and burned-out slagheap of a

country, it was usually shunned even by the Apaches. Its surface was torn and blistered by seams and craters from age-old volcanic upheavals. Later on it had been convulsed by earthquakes, polished by the wearing of rains. Cholla and bisnaga and ocotillo laced it; occasional cougars and coyote, antelope and bighorn sheep roamed its splintered fields.

Sunset seared the horizon like a red-hot bar of iron. Twilight began misting toward dusk. His charges were grumbling and cursing more loudly at each yard, and it was nearly time to call a halt.

Purdy said: "Pike, for Christ's sake!"

"All right. In a minute."

He chose a steep pocket in the shattered terrain. It would hide a fire, and a fire would do something for their spirits. They all slumped to the ground, looking glass-eyed and faintly stunned. By the time he'd assembled brush and had a small fire going, they began to stir a little. Purdy broke out the last of some beef sandwiches: "They'll spoil pretty quick — might well finish 'em up."

Severn lounged against a smooth boulder, arms folded, and languidly gave Twill orders regarding his comfort. So tired from bagtoting he could hardly walk, the big Negro moved stiffly to obey, laying out a blanket for the Southern gentleman to rest on, then fetching him a sandwich.

Yuma didn't understand it. Twill was built like a workhorse right enough, but he was also handsome, mannered, educated. Yet here he was, a man in his late thirties running errands, swallowing all kinds of abasement, flunkying like some levee-bred darkie who couldn't write his own name. Did blackness count that much against a man, even ability and schooling couldn't improve his lot? Yuma supposed so. He remembered the whip scars: Twill must have been a slave. Then they'd freed him to be half a man. . . .

Purdy tramped over and hunkered down by the fire. "How you advise we ration the water?"

"About a half cup apiece," Yuma said. "Another half cup for each come morning."

"That'll about finish her. How far's the Tanks from where we are?"

"We'll reach 'em around mid-morning tomorrow."

"We'll need to." Purdy took out his knife and plug cut, shaved off a wad and stowed it in his cheek, then licked the blade clean. "Just hope to Tophet there's water in 'em."

"I seen hotter summers they stayed wet."

Severn sauntered over, munching a sandwich. "How long d'you think we'll be reaching Silverton?" he asked.

Yuma shrugged. "Never tried walking it before, not with a passel of tenderfeet in tow. Three days . . . four."

Purdy squinted up at the Southerner. "You been pretty anxious. Can a man ask why?"

"It's hardly a secret." Severn touched his mustache. "Some years ago, my family was dispossessed. An accumulation of debts after the war — we lost everything we owned in Georgia. Most of us sought new fortunes in the West. My older brother had salvaged a little capital; he invested in San Francisco shipping and reaped handsome profits. A few days ago, I received word that he'd died leaving a highly contestable will. All the potential heirs, myself included, are converging on the West Coast for probate proceedings. There's a west-running spur train out of Silverton . . . understandably, I find any delay quite onerous. I hope all of this isn't over your head, Mr. Pike."

Yuma poked at the fire. "Not quite. I seen vultures gather."

Severn grinned superciliously. "That's fine. Poor as a rat and no itch for improvement, I take it."

"Only itch I got is in my foot, and money

89

don't scratch it."

"Fortunate man," Severn said lightly, and walked away.

Beth Ann Slaughter was lying on her side, quietly moaning, her face turned away from the others. She was too exhausted to raise another hysterical fuss, and that was a relief. The Duchess' shoes were coming apart; she was trying to patch them with sewing materials from her carpetbag. Getting up now, she came over to Beth Ann and sat down beside her, saying a few words of comfort. The girl never stirred or looked up, just continued her plaintive lowing.

"Come on," the Duchess said brusquely, "buck up. You sound like a pregnant cat about to deliver. Here . . . here's something'll help."

Flipping up her skirt edge, she pulled a small flat flask from a pocket in the hem of her petticoat. Yuma was vaguely familiar with the purpose of such pockets; generally ladies carried smelling salts in them. But the Duchess' flask didn't contain smelling salts. She slipped an arm under Beth Ann's shoulders and raised her enough to tilt the flask to her lips.

"Emergency ration. Take a nice big swallow, honey. Never had one before? I envy you. Come on, swallow . . . there's a real trooper. Sure it burns, you little boobie. You'll feel lovely in a minute. I'll have one myself before I perish of envy."

Sarge ran his tongue over his lower lip, his eyes following the flask from one mouth to the other. "Duchess, you belt away that Irish milk like a man do. Wouldn't have another of them handy little pockets some'eres, would you?"

"If I have, Mulrooney, you'll never see it. Here —" She capped the flask and tossed it across to him. "On me."

"Good old Duchess. Always a sport."

You could tell what liquor was to Sarge by the fevered way he held the flask, hands shaking. He drained it in a few long swallows. A different look came to his broad face: it relaxed expansively, almost foolishly, as if the nerve fibers had been gently severed. He walked around awhile, chuckling, smacking his hands together, humming to himself. Finally he swaggered over to the fire, leering at Yuma.

"Didn't mean nothing, all that rough talk a spell back. Hell, I got nothing against a siwash who's peaceable. Hope you'll disremember I said it, boy."

"Already forgot it, *boy.*"

Sarge cackled hoarsely and dropped down on his haunches beside Purdy, almost falling in the fire.

The Duchess held Beth Ann's hand till the girl drifted to sleep, which was in a few minutes. Getting up then, she went back to her shoes, seated herself cross-legged and continued her efforts to mend them. But the leather was tearing away from the soles; it was an impossible job.

"If I had a knife . . . may I borrow yours, Mr. Pike?"

Yuma got up and walked over, handing it to her. She raised her brows. "Well . . . never saw a knife like this one."

"No knife. It's a Spanish dagger."

She turned it in her hands. "It's really beautiful."

It was eight wicked inches of inch-wide Toledo steel, straight as a ruled line, with the special taper that the old Iberian craftsman could give a blade. A blood trough was grooved in either side from guard to point. The bone hilt was of more recent Navajo workmanship, inset with silver and lapis lazuli.

"Where did you get it?"

"A gift."

"Some gift. You must treasure it."

He did. Not just for itself, but because it was his father's one and only gift to him. Cuchillo claimed he'd taken it from a famous grandee he'd killed in his youth. Maybe he had. He always bragged when he was drunk, and it was while drunk that he'd given his half-white son the dagger.

Kneading her underlip between her teeth, she tried to use the knifetip as a leather awl. "Know what? I don't think this'll work."

"Them shoes are too far gone for fixing," Yuma said. "I got a pair of moccasins in my possibles. You better try them."

He got the moccasins. The Duchess admired their Apache design, the double-thick parfleche soles and the stiff upcurling toes. She pulled her skirt and petticoats calf-high to draw on the moccasins. Enough of her sleek black-stockinged legs showed for him to tell, with a man's sureness, that they were long and beautiful. After thonging the moccasins tight around her ankles, she got up to walk across the camp and back.

"Say, these are just dandy." She grinned at him. "I won't even ask where you got 'em."

Yuma grinned back. She was quite a figure in the firelight: robust and full-breasted, as tall as he was, her thick maroon mass of hair catching fiery dribbles of light. And he could talk to her without awkwardness, which wasn't usual.

"That really your name . . . Duchess?"

"One of 'em. Roxanne Carroll, once of Baltimore. Later Mrs. Roxanne Harris. Then Roxy the Silver Thrush of Silver City — I sing, you know. Was tagged the 'Duchess' in Tubac where I ran a gaming house — gaming, not sporting — till the house got broke. Forcing me to examine, ahem, fresh prospects."

"No Mr. Harris now?"

"Mr. Harris deserted me eight years ago. A real sweetie. I mean really. He was considerate. Left me young enough that I still had the accessories to help make ends meet."

Yuma split the guard duty among himself and the other men. Not that he expected trouble tonight. The Apaches hadn't caught up and wouldn't attack if they had. Not and risk dying in the dark. What about tomorrow, though? It kept running through his brain as he lay awake, hands folded behind his head, while Purdy paced the first watch.

What if they couldn't reach the Tanks before Cipriano overhauled them? They'd have to make a fight. Bleakly he assessed his force. Sarge might be an old campaigner . . . but the rest? One thing, the people from the stage weren't shy on courage or they'd all have stayed in Tubac till the hostile trouble blew over. Courage, or plain ignorance. A lot of times, it seemed, the difference cut pretty fine.

The world was still muffled in the dead soft beige of pre-dawn when he roused them out to a chorus of grumbling and cursing, mostly from Sarge: "Hell's bells, ain't no need to pile out this early!"

"We want to cover ground while it holds cool. Come on, shake into it."

Full of cramps and soreness from yesterday's hike, they were a stiff-limbed and miserable crew as they tramped behind him, pushing steadily north. The gray light gentled the crabbed shape of the lava country. It was a little like tramping the face of a dead world, old and cratered and time-frozen, before the pearly blaze of real dawn picked out cacti and scrub brush, and a few birds started noising it up.

Sarge tramped up beside Yuma. "You got anything to smoke?"

"Nothing you'd fancy."

"How d'you know?"

Yuma passed him one of his Spanish cigars. Sarge peered at it, sniffed it, and stuck it in his teeth. He lighted up, said "Jesus" with a faint shudder, then smoked on gingerly. Yuma glanced back over his shoulder, scanning the serrated rim of land, then turned front again. He caught Sarge's red-rimmed glance.

"What you expect to see back there, boy?"

"Nothing."

"Why-for you keep looking around then? Specially backward?"

"Keeping alive seems a fair reason. When you don't see a thing is the time to watch."

Sarge grunted, screwing up his face like a colicky baby's. "Christ. I smoked mule turds that outshined your stogies."

"Never did myself."

After sunup, the heat increased quickly. In an hour they were all plodding slowly, stumbling a little. Purdy and Sarge took turns assisting the women. There was a drunken stagger to John Twill's stride. The portmanteaus swung like lead weights at the ends of his long arms; his shirt hung on his body like a wet filthy rag. Yuma called a rest halt and doled out the last of the canteen water. He measured out a half-cup into his own water flask, hesitated, then added another half-cup.

"One moment, my man," said Severn. "Each of us took only half a cup. If you wish to save yours, I'm sure nobody objects. But a full cup?"

"Mr. Twill's share and my share," Yuma said. "I'm giving it all to Mr. Twill. He'll need it if he carries your precious stuff much farther. Any objection?"

Severn smiled. "Of course not — if you want to sacrifice your own drink."

Twill had flung himself exhaustedly to the ground. He barely looked up as Yuma came over, squatted down, and held out the flask.

"Not your share, Mr. Pike."

"I wasn't going to drink anyways. You don't want it, I'll split 'er among the rest."

Twill's smile was a bone-white streak in his face. "You're fantastic, Mr. Pike." He took the water flask and emptied it in slow small sips.

Yuma said: "Look, tie them bags on my horse, why don't you?"

"Thank you. I can't do that; Mr. Severn wouldn't permit it."

"Why the hell not?"

"He wouldn't, that's all."

"Like your job, do you, Mr. Twill?"

"It's a job, Mr. Pike." Twill capped the empty flask and handed it back. "A colored man can't be picky. I shouldn't have to remind you."

"I dunno," Yuma said. "Always figured even a colored man had a choice. Live like a man or like a dog. Up to him."

Twill sighed and leaned back against a rock, lacing his hands across his stomach. "I was quite fortunate when I was a pick-

97

aninny. I was one year old when Mas'r's son was born; I was chosen to be Mister Davey's lifelong bodyservant. I was taken away from Nigger Row and raised with Mister Davey up in the big house. When Mas'r brought special tutors from abroad to educate his son, a good deal rubbed off on me. *Je peux à peu près me faire comprendre en français.* And I speak English rather well, don't you think?"

"Middling."

Twill smiled faintly. "When the war was over and nominal freedom was ours, I was sixteen. Mas'r's fortune was wiped out and he couldn't afford even to feed his darkies, much less pay them as the law required. I returned to my parents, we tried to eke out a living on a few acres of backwoods dust. Red Georgia dust . . . it blew all day and nothing grew. We were starving and a white farmer had chickens, hundreds of chickens. One night a few of us raided his coops. We got three chickens. Next night some white-sheet fellows — gentlemen from their voices, and drunk — called on our shanty row. They took out the head of each family and hanged him to a tree. They took out the eldest sons of each family and tied them to other trees and used bullwhips on their backs. Then they burned a cross and left."

Twill's hands had clenched together till the veins stood out in knots. He looked down at his hands and unlaced his fingers. "I was my father's only son."

"Noticed the scars."

"That was the night I learned what's been restated for me many times since. There really is no choice for a man of color. None at all."

"There's one," Yuma said. Twill raised his brows, and Yuma added: "Freedom or death . . . if it comes to that. Men've gone out on battlefields and died for a lot less reason."

"I think there's a difference, Mr. Pike. A soldier risks death for a cause — his ideals, his country, his family — and if he dies, others will carry on his fight." He spread his hands. "Any defiance of mine would be an empty gesture. My people have been cowed too long; they won't fight. Individuals — yes. A Nat Turner here and there. All died. And their deaths, like the sporadic outbursts of your Indian bands, accomplished nothing. What a futility!"

"I ain't talking about your people." Yuma jabbed a finger at him. "I'm talking about you. You as a man. You alone. What do *you* decide?"

"That a live lackey is better than a dead fool."

"Well then, Mr. Twill —" Yuma rose to his feet. "You're dead already. Maybe I'll have the job of burying you. That's about all that's left, ain't it?"

He tramped away, swinging his arm in a brusque motion that made the others climb stiffly to their feet.

"You're pushing sort of hard, Pike," Purdy grunted. "Hope them Tanks ain't much farther."

"Less'n an hour if we get a move on."

As he spoke, Yuma scanned their back route again. No movement in all that brick-tan desolation. Not yet. As he swung back to lead the way, he felt Sarge's hard quizzical glance touch him once more.

CHAPTER SIX

They tramped. The sun flamed and pressured their bodies like wet boiling-hot cotton. Heat shimmered in flat pools below the horizon like far-off lakes. A loaflike ridge took form out of the anonymous swells of land, a basalt-dark ridge that stood sharp against those surrounding it.

"Almost there," Yuma said. "Other side of that ridge."

At that moment, John Twill missed a wobbling step and fell, plowing into the ground on his face. He climbed to his hands and knees, slowly shaking his head. The others halted and watched him. Twill raised his dust-caked face.

"Mr. Severn . . . I'm sorry, sir. I can't make it."

"Come along; you heard Pike. Just a bit farther."

"I'm sorry, sir. I can't carry those bags even a yard further."

Severn's sun-glazed eyes narrowed. "Let's not have any nonsense. Pick up the bags."

Still on his hands and knees, Twill met his stare for a long moment. Then he rose to his feet with a labored, pain-wracked slowness. "No, sir. I don't think I will."

"Oh, you will," Severn said softly. "Make no mistake. You'll pick them up!"

Twill straightened his shoulders. "I think not, sir. Not unless I'm working for you. So — as of this moment, I am leaving your service."

"Ho, that's telling this fine bird," Sarge chuckled. "Lay it to him, Uncle!"

Severn's hand snaked to his belt and up. Sun glinted on blued pistol steel. "You're through when I tell you. Now you damned insolent black beggar, pick up those bags."

"No, sir." Twill hesitated, sweat streaking down his dusty face. "I'll be damned if I will."

The trigger-guard lever of Yuma's Sharps made a brittle-dry cocking as he turned on his heel. When he stopped, the barrel was leveled at Severn's belly.

"How much are your possibles worth to you, Mr. Severn?"

Severn's laugh was cold and quiet. "Very well." He let his pistol off-cock and sheathed it. "John, where I was raised, a nigger jumps when he's told. He keeps his place or he learns why he should have. I trust it was the same where you were raised."

"It was, sir. But we're no longer there, you or I."

"No. But we're the same men, John. Our places remain as stated. You're going to learn about that." Severn shuttled a half-lidded glance to Yuma. "Your half-breed friend's gun won't stand between us when I choose to drive the lesson home. And I will, John. I promise you."

Yuma motioned slightly with the Sharps, turned on his heel and tramped away. The others moved into step behind him, except for Severn. The Southerner picked up one of his bags, then the other, before following them. In a few minutes he was falling behind, cursing and sweating. Finally he dropped to his knees.

"Wait a minute! I want to repack . . . throw away some of these things and put the rest in one bag —"

"You can catch up," Yuma said, not breaking stride. Severn swore at him. They swung on, leaving Severn on his knees dumping out the portmanteaus. The land climbed. Bluish-black shoulders of basalt began to grow beyond the skyline, and these marked the Redondo Tanks.

Yuma stopped suddenly and swung around. He wasn't sure why, but he knew as he turned, his eyes crossing a smudgy shroud of dust coming low against the land swells south.

Too late. Cipriano. It had to be.

The others came around too, looking, not tightening at once on the faint haze that was plain as writing to his eye, but seeing it then and all eyes turning on Yuma. He swung his head toward the rim of basalt. There was — not escape, but protection. The huge-slabbed rocks that surrounded the Tanks would provide it. But they were too far away, he knew with a savage certainty. Afoot and fagged out already, they couldn't make it.

A lot of smaller but more exposed rocks

103

stood out in a loose field ahead of the Tanks. It wasn't good cover, but if they could get that far, they could retreat through the rocks to the Tanks with the help of a covering fire.

"Pike?" Purdy said.

" 'Paches sure."

Purdy's eyes slitted hard at him. "You have an idea they'd follow us this far?"

"Always a chance of it. Come on!"

A slow trot was the best they could manage. The two women were almost done in; Severn staggered in a weaving line clutching his bag. Yuma helped the Duchess — Roxanne — along, his hand tight on her arm while he constantly checked the Apaches' progress. The dust cloud had already sprinkled apart into dark separate figures, coming fast.

"We'll never make it!" Roxanne was stumbling, almost falling, as he pulled her along. "Go on . . . your horse . . . why should you stay? You could get out!"

"Maybe."

"You don't owe us anything!"

They were close to the rocks, they would make it, but the Apaches were a lot nearer now, the warriors hanging low to their ponies' withers, coming across quite open terrain and their prey plain ahead of them. Yuma, holding Roxanne with one arm, pulling the horses along with the other, led his companions into the rocks. He halted just long enough to unfasten the rifles from his saddle and pass them around to the men; he hastily distributed ammunition too.

The Apaches were almost into the rocks now; some were already piling off their horses, plunging forward, a few of them firing. Sarge wheeled and dropped to one knee, raising his pistol straight-armed and pumping shots. The Apaches were scattering widely through the rocks, fanning quickly out as if to overtake and enclose them. Twill fell back beside Sarge to lend a fire of his own, but Sarge roared: "Get your black hide gone, Uncle! It's my party!"

Twill looked rather helplessly at the rifle in his hands, then ran after the others. Severn hesitated, threw his bag aside and came back to drop down beside Sarge. The old soldier sent him one look, then the two of them were hammering a covering fire at the enemy, shielding the others' retreat: Yuma with the horses and Roxanne, Purdy helping Beth Ann along, Twill following.

The Apaches fanning through the rocks were stopped cold. Not that there was much to fire at: dark flitting shapes, a painted face here, a coppery arm there, momentary targets. One was hit and went down with a keening yell.

Sarge and Severn began to fall slowly back, following the others. But the situation was still tight: the warriors that were still mounted had surged apart in two loose waves, and the waves were pounding on through the boulder field, their bodies swung down from sight as they hugged their ponies' off flanks. No targets there.

Their intention was clear: swing around and past their enemies, get between them and the Tanks, cut them off, pin them in the poor cover of the rock field, then surround and cut them to pieces.

Yuma pulled up hard on his heels, ready to swing up his hand and yell for the others to stop and dig in where they were.

He didn't get the words out. An Apache pony swinging past the basalt rim of the Tanks suddenly went down in a kicking sprawl, head-shot. His rider somersaulted on the ground, started to get up and was smashed back by a second bullet.

There was a harsh peppering fire all around; Yuma couldn't isolate those two shot sounds. But his eyes sought instinctively beyond the downed pony and rider — the shot had come from the Tanks side — and he saw powdersmoke bloom among the boulders.

Somebody was already at the Tanks. Friendly. He was shooting at the Apaches, and he had caught them sudden and exposed on that side. His next shot sent a second pony to the ground, and when the rider floundered up, he was picked off as neatly as the first.

The warriors were sandwiched between two fires. They couldn't stand the gaff, and Cipriano knew it: Yuma heard his voice raging at them to pull off, pull back.

Yuma hugged a rock and, Sharps raised and cocked, strained his eyes at the dust moil raised by the Apache ponies, trying to pick out Cipriano. But the dust was too heavy; it bannered even thicker as the yelling Apaches wheeled and bolted away from the Tanks and the crippling fire: they were all open on that side, and the rifleman knocked another from his pony. He staggered to his feet: another warrior wheeled back and dipped an arm and swung him up behind. They followed the others into the yellow obscurity of the dust.

The way to the Tanks was open.

Yuma dragged Roxanne to her feet and hurried, and the others crowded behind him, Sarge and Severn still firing occasionally at the Apaches in the rocks.

A man moved into sight from behind the

basalt, stepping onto a high rock. He raised his rifle above his head and waved it, motioning them in. Then he came down off the rock and stood waiting. The horses scented water, and Yuma let them go and they trotted in past the shouldering lava and into the shallow arroyo that cupped the three rock-enclosed pools which gave Redondo Tanks its name.

They were close enough to see the man clearly; Purdy said: "It's Tony Avila, sure."

"Who's he?" Yuma asked.

"Deputy sheriff up at Salazar."

"I know the place. Thirty-forty Mexicans work some mines there."

"Yeah. Wonder what brings him this far south?"

They reached the arroyo edge and Avila motioned them down into its shelter. The main catch basin was almost squarely in the center of the arroyo, the water three to four feet deep and shaded by sloping lava walls. Toward the upper end of the arroyo where its walls almost pinched off lay another pool, smaller and even more confined; and down below the main tank was another, the arroyo wider here and scattered thickly with boulders.

"How, Tony."

"Crim. You lost your stage maybe?"

"Back yesterday," Purdy said. "This here's Yuma Pike. Tony Avila."

Avila was slender and olive-skinned, maybe forty-five, with a potty hint of paunch and a graying black mustache. His black eyes sparkled mournfully, socketed deep in his round head. The baggy black suit he wore was limp and gray with trail dust. He looked mildly worried, a little soft, a little too old to enjoy his job, but he was a good man, a competent hand — that was how Yuma sized him.

When the others had slaked their thirsts at the big tank, Purdy introduced them; Avila politely raised his hat to the women.

"Man," Purdy said then, "what're you doing this far down, and way off the Salazar road? Ain't you heard Cipriano is out."

"Cipriano? He has broken again?"

"Sure; good five days ago. Cutting a goodly swath south. We was hit and set afoot about halfway between Silverton and Tubac. Not much water, and Pike here opined our best bet was the Tanks, so we lit out for here. Surprised you ain't heard about Cipriano."

Avila shrugged. "You know how far Salazar is from much of any place. Buried in the hills, and the road in don't lead nowhere except to Salazar. One supply train every two weeks, and never a traveler along to bring news."

"I reckon. But why you way over here off the beat track?"

Avila motioned, and they followed him across the trampled ground around the big tank to a rocky niche under the arroyo bank. A man lay curled up on his side in the shade there. His hands were handcuffed behind his back and a sombrero was tilted across his face; he was sleeping or just resting.

"He's my reason," Avila said.

Purdy grunted. "Who is he?"

"Cayetano Tamargo. He tried to rob the payroll safe at the mine office, but he made a mistake. Now I'm taking him in for trial."

"To Tubac?"

"That's where the county seat is, where the sheriff's office is, where the circuit judge presides. I'm only the deputy at Salazar, and the judge don't come there. So, this Tamargo is a dangerous fellow, I figure I better get him to Tubac quick. You know the Salazar road, how it goes all over the mountains and way up to Bleekerstown before there's a road cuts south to Tubac. So I figure cut across country pretty straight, travel light and fast, lay over at Redondo Tanks a half day, then down to the road and flag a stage. But no more stages for awhile, eh?"

Purdy shook his head. "They cut off the runs. I was making a special one. We figured to cut from here straight across to Tubac."

The man curled on the ground sat up slowly, kind of unwinding as he did. Cayetano Tamargo was long, and he undulated when he moved, like a cat or a big brown rattler. If he stood, he would probably be three or four inches above six feet. He raised up his head. It was like a wedge, with gaunt jaws scooping down to the apex of a shelving chin. His skin was leather-burned; his eyes were old eyes, old as sin though he wasn't over thirty, and they were blue with the blood of Old Spain and as cold as pond ice. Faintly, something twinkling and debonair touched them, and his thin lips curled with wry derision, like a shadow of some wasted elegance. He dressed all in brown leather, sombrero and jacket and tight trousers, all *charro*-trimmed.

"*Buenos días,*" he said politely.

"Morning," Purdy said. He looked at Avila. "We best get set up here. I don't reckon Cipriano is done with us by a wide shot. Pike, here, sort of knows the 'paches and he's led us this far. I 'low we better let him give all the orders, if that's all right with you."

"Yes." Tamargo laughed, scanning Yuma's face. "He'd know the Apache, this one. It shows. You do what he says, Antonio. The *Indios* should stick together."

"Shut up, Cayetano," Avila said. "I don't give a damn for your proud blood. It has gone stinking." His mournful gaze touched Yuma's. "If you know the Apach', if Crim Purdy trusts you, that is good enough for me. What do we do?"

CHAPTER SEVEN

No sign of Apaches now. The heat-rippled flats looked deserted on all sides. But an attack could come any time, any number of ways. So Yuma's first move was to inspect their position, then assign posts to each man. Maybe fifty feet across its broad lower end, the arroyo covered a lot of ground for so few to defend. But it was rimmed on all sides by massive basalt thrusts that would provide pretty fair cover for the defenders. The basalt slabs were too high to be easily scaled, the gaps between them mostly choked by brush. You could only find easy access to the arroyo at a few places; these would be easily covered.

What worried Yuma most were the loosely scattered boulders and heavy mattings of

112

brush that laced the flat ground on each flank of the natural fort: limited cover for the Apaches if they tried to move in close. He sized up the likeliest approaches, where boulders lay thickest beyond their rock cordon and gaps in the cordon itself, and spaced the men at rough intervals along the arroyo flanks, cautioning them to watch the approaches. Afterward he watered their horses at the lowest tank. A little rest, water and forage, and both animals should be all right.

Purdy was stationed a few yards away, covering the arroyo's lower end. He ran his tongue over his cracked underlip, squinting across the empty flats. "Reckon they ain't about to rush us without they're blamed sure. Ain't that the 'pache way?"

Yuma shrugged. " 'Pache way is any way that works best. Cipriano ain't likely to ride all his chips on one deal. Likely he'll try whittling us down, picking us off. When he's cut his odds low enough. . . ."

"Christ." Purdy spat unhappily at a rock. "They come at us by night, they'll come through them rocks like shadows."

"Night attack ain't too likely, but I'll make 'em out all right." Yuma's glance moved to a cluster of tall rocks that walled the pinched-off upper tip of the wash. "Fair lookout point there. I'll keep a watch."

Sarge, who was posted halfway up the arroyo, heaved around to give Yuma a hard grin. "Boy, you know a sight about everything them siwashes do. Too goddam much to sit easy in my craw."

"Maybe enough to keep us alive too," Purdy growled. "Why'n't you lay off him?"

"Don't get your ass in an uproar, Mr. Purdy. Just wondering." Sarge sleeved his red sweating face, holding the grinning stare on Yuma. "Like how he knowed Cipriano would follar us fast and straight like he done."

"Maybe I just didn't," Yuma said. "Maybe keeping an eye peeled helps. How many more ways you want me to say it?"

"I ain't asking. Just got a feeling you knowed it all along. Knowed it plain as ticks on a bare-ass mule."

Yuma swung one foot enough to heel around, coming full-face to the ex-soldier. "You might make that a whole lot plainer," he said gently.

"Not yet," Sarge grinned. "I just gonna keep my eye peeled too, boy. On you."

Yuma let it go at that. He tramped the length of the arroyo, checking each man's position. Beth Ann Slaughter was stretched on a blanket by the middle tank, a wet cloth

114

over her face. The Duchess sat beside her, exhausted and fine-drawn but still chipper; she gave Yuma a solemn wink.

"Hey. Man with the magic. How about digging up a rifle for me?"

"Fresh out," Yuma said. "Keep your head down."

"Don't worry."

He came to John Twill who sat on a rock with one of the Apache Winchesters in his hands, looking embarrassed. "Perhaps the lady should take mine. I never held one of these . . . can't even load it."

Yuma took it from him and explained the weapon from butt to barrel. "Snug it to your shoulder like this, aim and squeeze off. They get close enough, you could get lucky."

"Or vice versa," Twill said wryly.

Moving on, Yuma noted the tracks of bighorn sheep in the loose soil around the basins. Cougar, coyote and antelope had also watered here. But none would come to drink while people remained. Mesquite beans and random puff balls grew in the arroyo; while they lasted, these would answer for food. Quail sign was plentiful around the brushy places; he could rig a few snares later on. Water was the main concern, and they had plenty. The Apaches would have little or none, but they'd make out. They always did.

"I say . . . Pike."

Severn was at his post by a basalt slab; he mopped his face with a grimy handkerchief and gave Yuma a kind of unfocused glare. He was dirty and disheveled, his air of cool composure starting to disintegrate around the edges. Yuma tramped over to him.

"Do you think it wise to just sit and wait for them?"

"You got a better idea?"

"We have four horses, haven't we? Your two are done in, but the ones belonging to these Mexican fellows look fairly fresh." Severn nodded at the tall bay and runty rugged pinto tethered by an ocotillo clump. "Couldn't a couple of us try a break? If one got through, he might bring help."

Cayetano Tamargo was curled up in his rock shade close by, somnolent as a brown lizard. His handcuffs rattled as he raised his hands, tipping his sombrero back off his eyes. *"Stupido,"* he murmured.

"So much for the bandido cheering section." Severn smiled thinly. "My notion is, one man might ride out and provide a distraction. Giving the second a chance to make it through."

A chuckle rippled up from Tamargo's chest. "Me, I think that is damn pretty idea.

116

Hey — you, gentleman. Maybe you be the one who go first, hey?"

"Of course. I'll take the risk. If you'll second me, Pike?"

"Ho!" Tamargo laughed. "Hey, gentleman. That big horse. The bay — eh? He is mine. Now I give him to you. You take him and go out first. I think you be damn quick dead."

"We both would," Yuma said. "It won't fool Cipriano."

Severn straightened, a cool blaze in his eyes. Yuma didn't like the look: he sensed that the Southerner's reckless mood leaned harder toward desperation than courage.

"Then I'll go alone. And damn you for a coward, Pike."

"I ain't disposed to argue," Yuma said mildly. "You ain't riding out, though."

"You heard him. The horse is mine."

"It ain't his to give. There's nine of us here, mister, and only four horses. We're all in the same tight, and that makes the horses common property."

Severn's voice was rigidly controlled. "By your lights, perhaps."

"Hey." Tamargo rolled catlike to his haunches, winking. "That's right. His. You don't take orders from no breed, eh? Me neither." He tapped a thumb against his chest. "Me, Tamargo, I give you the horse. The breed, he has no say."

Avila walked up at his stocky, rolling stride. He thrust his rifle under Tamargo's chin. "Listen, Cayetano. You keep your face shut, *comprende?* Or I let this thing off in your throat."

Tamargo lay back, chuckling. "Sure, Antonio. It's what you say."

Avila had halted between Yuma and Severn. It was a casual but deliberate gesture that had the effect, somehow, of crushing the tension. Now Avila glanced at Severn, saying politely: "He's my prisoner; he has no rights. So the horse he can't give you."

Severn was still stiff and hot-eyed. "And you agree with Pike, I suppose?"

"In this, yes. I know the Apach'. Not so good as this man maybe. But enough I can tell you that you ride out, you alone or two of us or three, it makes no difference. The Apach' will get us all." Avila's dark eyes flicked to Yuma. "This is by day. But maybe after dark, there is a chance, eh?"

Yuma shook his head. "I might make it. None of you would."

He said it with a flat conviction. Avila blinked and nodded slowly.

"All right," he said, "I believe you. Maybe if we hold out awhile, one, two days, there

118

will be help. Word will reach Tubac that a stage went out. People will come looking — a big well-armed force that won't be afraid of running into the Apach'. They will pick up the tracks — they will guess to come here."

"Maybe," Yuma said. "But not in one or two days. This stage was a special run; it won't be expected. When word does come through, they'll be a spell working up to what they'll do. Some will say if they wait, we'll come in by ourselves; if we don't, it'll be too late anyways. All right. Allow three, four days for word to get through, a couple more for 'em to make up their minds. By then. . . ."

"It is all over," Avila said in a calm hollow tone.

"All I'm saying, don't count on outside help. If there's a way out, and maybe there is, it ain't likely to come from that quarter."

"You said you could make it by night," Severn pointed out coldly.

"Might sneak out on foot. But not horseback. Come dawn, they'd find my track and run me down."

"Ah." Severn was immensely sarcastic. "Then we simply wait . . . and how long can we afford to simply wait?"

"I'll let you know."

Yuma turned on his heel and walked back to the horses. Ease down, he told himself. Don't let 'em needle you. He pulled his knife and began hacking down stalks of ocotillo and small brush. If the horses were to be any use, they had to be kept alive and in sound shape, and they had to be kept from spooking and bolting if things got too warm. A makeshift corral built in some sheltering rocks would do the trick. There was scanty forage available — galleta grass and mesquite beans — but it would stretch pretty fine among four animals.

Roxanne got up and came over to him. She leaned her hip against a rock and folded her arms. "What's that for?"

"A corral, sort of."

"Don't let them rawhide you . . . Sarge and that bogus gentleman."

"They're a pair to scrape a body fine."

"Don't I know it. I had a place in Silverton — very up and up, booze and cards and ladies, but no back rooms — and those two were among my sterling customers. Mr. Severn makes much of his fallen fortunes, but he's too much at home with a deck of cards and that shiny little cannon he packs to be altogether wool and a yard wide. I think he belly-stripped sometimes, but nobody ever proved it. He made a living playing poker and kicked up a little trouble now and then, and I think he rather enjoyed the whole business."

"How about the soldier?"

"Sarge? He's a bummer; he moves around. Cashiered after his arm was amputated. An Apache arrow did it. I guess he's not too charitable about the breed, if you'll pardon a manner of speaking."

Yuma straightened up, sleeving sweat off his forehead. He looked at her. "That leaves you."

"A setup turns stale sometimes; you move along." She shrugged her shoulders. "Nothing else to it." Her face changed slightly. "There was someone I trusted and shouldn't have. Part of it, I suppose."

"A man?"

"Man. Men. What's the difference?" Her voice turned faintly acrid. "I've known enough of 'em, and what's it got me? I don't even benefit from experience."

Yuma gathered up an armful of cuttings and dumped them between a pair of slabs that formed a deep nook. "Depends what you're really looking for."

"Does it? You know what you're looking for?"

"I got all I want."

"Have you." Her green eyes deepened

with a soft mockery. "Freedom, that is?"

"I reckon."

The Duchess laughed. "Don't fool yourself, friend. You're here, aren't you? You've stuck by us. Out of, I presume, a sense of obligation — a bow to humanity. An obliged man just isn't free."

"Things get tight, I can always clear out."

"The devil you can." She straightened away from the rock, grinning with the friendliest sort of derision. "Or if you can — the devil you *will.*"

She laughed at him and sauntered away.

He began weaving brush and ocotillo stalks together into loose quick twists, building an interlaced barrier between the slabs. The zebra dun whickered and nuzzled at his elbow; he gave the animal's muzzle a speculative rub.

Was the Duchess right? A fine wire of anticipation tightened around his belly: in a few hours the zebra dun should be rested, strong as ever, ready for anything. There was a chance, maybe the thinnest of chances, that a sudden dash would carry the dun and him through a scattered siege line of warriors. Once beyond and away, they'd outrun the best Apache ponies. . . .

And failing to catch him, Cipriano would vent his fury on those who remained. One gun less, shorn of whatever value his leadership had meant, they'd be that much easier prey. Whatever help he could muster at Tubac would come too late.

Yuma left an opening in the barrier to drive the horses through and, once they were inside, heaped a mass of brush across the breach to confine them. Afterward he picked up his rifle and walked back to the bottleneck end of the wash, climbing the clustered rocks he'd chosen for a lookout.

He was hardly settled when the Apaches made their move.

It wasn't a concerted charge. Just a sudden scatter of dusky forms coming through rocks and cholla and mesquite, running in short zigzag sprints. A few of them fired shots before dropping out of sight. By the time the men in the arroyo were returning fire, there was nothing to fire at.

It went that way for the next few minutes: the Apaches making a game of it, lifting up and charging a few feet and melting to the ground again. For the defenders, it meant shooting at ghosts. When some few warriors had gotten within fifty yards of the arroyo, someone gave a shrill whistle. The attack, such as it was, broke off altogether.

This had been only a ploy to feel them out, Yuma guessed. Knowing they were ready, Cipriano wouldn't press too hard. Not right away. He would let the pressure of blasting heat and waiting and strained nerves work on them for awhile. . . .

Time dragged by. There was a sparse exchange of shots. Now and then an Apache would spring up and charge, a dim running target in the fog of brush. By the time someone drew a bead, he would be gone. One warrior was particularly foolhardy. He kept leaping from one position to the next, letting out taunting yips. He had a rich vocabulary of Spanish invective and a limping command of English cuss words, and he made voluble use of both. Finally Sarge lost his temper and, savagely cursing, emptied his rifle into a clump of brush where the taunter should have been but wasn't.

Yuma shifted on his haunches. "Save it!" he yelled.

"Shut your Christ-bitten siwash mouth!" Sarge yelled back.

Their voices rolled into a hot trailing silence. Nothing more was said. The sun blazed fiercely into the arroyo. Crouched among baking boulders, Yuma felt the sweat glide down his ribs and puddle in his boots. He kept his cheek snugged against his rifle stock, watching. From his high position he caught occasional suspicions of movement the others didn't, yet he held his fire. An aching band of strain across his neck and shoulders made him aware of his tension: he rocked back on his heels, forcing his muscles to relax.

If he could pick out Cipriano . . . if he could once get a bead on Cipriano.

The spry taunter made another short dash and plunged out of sight again. "Son bitch! Son bitch!" he jeered at them, singsonging the words.

Yuma studied the slant of a flat-sided boulder looming over the brush-choked knoll where the buck had disappeared. Maybe, he thought, and eased the rifle to his shoulder, taking a hair-fine aim on the rock. He squeezed trigger. The ricochetting bullet sang; the Apache yelped and leaped up, blood streaking his face.

Purdy and Severn fired, the shots merging. The Apache was slammed against the flat rock. For a moment he hung as if pinned there, then fell forward.

With full-throated shouts of rage, the Apaches began shooting in earnest. Three warriors surged out of cover. Yuma shot one in the belly, knocking him back to the ground in a kicking sprawl. A horse, mortally hit, let out a high whickering scream.

The shooting slacked off swiftly. Again,

125

suddenly, the rock field was empty. The wounded horse was making high-pitched squeals. Twill hurried over to the brush corral and peered inside. His gleaming face swung toward Yuma.

"One was hit, Mr. Pike . . . a ricochet it must have been."

"Finish him off."

Twill's eyes were wide and staring. He turned slowly around, awkwardly levering his rifle, and pushed the muzzle over the barrier. His whole body jerked with the shot. He backed away, dropped to his knees, bent his face almost to the ground and vomited.

Severn gave a contemptuous bark of laughter. "Good boy, John."

"Pike!"

Roxanne Harris said his name. Her voice was soft, sharp, almost hushed, but it yanked Yuma's gaze from the rock field and brought him around. The Duchess was at Tony Avila's side. The lawman was braced against a boulder and slipping toward the ground, supported only by Roxanne's arms. Avila's olive complexion was gray with shock and pain, his hands grabbing his chest. Blood ran between his fingers.

"Oh God . . . oh God!" Beth Ann Slaughter crawled to her knees, staring at Avila.

"We're going to die here. All of us. *We're going to die!*"

Her screamed words pounded against the cordon of huge-slabbed rocks, clawing a few shallow echoes from them. Nothing else gave back an answer. . . .

CHAPTER EIGHT

Late afternoon had flung elongated shadows across the arroyo. Sprawled on his back in the rock shade, hands folded under his head, Cayetano Tamargo resembled a gaunt cougar taking its ease. He studied the others through half-shuttered eyes. His gaze rested longest on the woman, Roxanne and on the breed, Yuma Pike.

The breed was whipping together a meal of sorts. He had snared a brace of quail by rigging a few running nooses in the arching masses of brush at the arroyo's west flank. He had sliced up a puffball for frying and brewed up a revolting coffee from mesquite beans. Lean fare to stretch among so many, but it would take the edge off hunger; it would keep their strength at fighting level.

He was a man to reckon with, this Pike. The gringos, knowing it too, looked to his leadership whether they liked it or not. Even the three who distrusted him, Severn and

Mulrooney and the Slaughter *chica*, had swallowed their color-hate sufficiently to accept him that far. For now, at least.

The pale ninny of a Slaughter *chica* continued to huddle on the ground, whimpering that she didn't want to die. As if anyone did. The others ignored her. Tamargo listened with a lazy irritation to her sobbing and thought how good it would be to shut off her throat with his strong fingers and end her banal whining.

His glance stirred to Avila, who lay on a blanket in the deep shade not ten yards away. Avila's eyes were closed, his face puffy and loose, his skin flush-mottled with fever. His shirt was open, his thick chest bandaged with strips from one of Roxanne's torn-up petticoats; blood spotted the cloth. He was hit very bad, Antonio. Maybe he would not live. It was too bad. He was a good man, simple, devoted to his duty, therefore something of a fool by Tamargo's standards. Still, he had risked his life to save Tamargo from the miner scum who had sought to string him up, just as he'd doggedly undertaken to deliver his prisoner to Tubac and a fair trial. Ah, yes; a good man, as Tamargo's own father had been good.

Cayetano grinned, his mouth twisting with a small damp fury. That *cabrón* of a *hacendado* who had claimed that the Tamargos were squatters and had sent his *vaqueros* to run them off, as if they were no better than the common run of ragged *peónes*. As if, shrunken in land and goods, they were not still of the pure blood, the best of old Aragon. Tamargo's father and two brothers had been killed in the ensuing fight. Cayetano had escaped. That night he had gone to the *hacienda;* he had left Don Luis on the floor of his great *casa* in a pool of his own blood. Sonora . . . ten years ago. But the fat price on his head stood today, and he had never returned.

It was not a bad life. He had his pearl-handled gold-inlaid pistol, his silver-trimmed saddle and a fast bay horse, and no scruples at all. What more did a man need to make his way? It had been not at all bad while it lasted, but maybe it was no more. He had counted, during the long ride to Tubac, on finding a way to overcome Avila and escape. *A Dios,* Antonio! But the Apach' out there, they were something else, and so maybe it was ended.

He dug his rump into the cool ground, rolling his hips for comfort. His manacled wrists were chafed raw. *Es barbaridad!* He felt like a trussed pig. It was no way to die.

It had gone on all afternoon: the sporadic

bursts of gunfire, the occasional arrow, the isolated sniper shots. The long nerve-tearing silences between. There was little else to be seen or heard out beyond the arroyo. Even the bodies of the two dead Apaches had miraculously vanished. . . .

Antonio had packed some cooking utensils on his saddle: a skillet and a coffeepot, also two plates and two cups. Pike had prepared the food; Roxanne dished up the slim fare and distributed it to the men at their stations around the rock cordon. They took turns with the plates and cups, shuddering as they swigged the awful brew. Severn complained loudly and said he refused to touch such slop.

"Señora!" Tamargo rolled up like a cat onto his haunches, a great smile splitting his face. "This one, he is happy to eat the slop from your beautiful hands. If you be so kind . . . hey?"

Roxanne glanced over at Pike; the breed shrugged. "He can have it."

She carried the plate over to Tamargo. His eyes admired her long-legged walk, her jade-colored eyes, and her hair that flamed in the sun, the fullness and beauty that even a limp and dirty traveling suit, seam-torn and full of brush-rips, couldn't dim. *Dios!* Nothing could dim such a woman.

130

"*Señora. . . .*" Avila's eyes were open, puffy-lidded with fever; his voice was reedy and faint. "Be careful with this one."

Cayetano chuckled. "Tell her, Antonio. Tell her how bad Tamargo is."

"I can guess," Roxanne said dryly.

"He killed a woman with his hands. It was never proved, but he knows. I know. Watch him."

"I'll bet he's full of surprises."

Tamargo showed all his teeth. "Such a beautiful tongue." He rattled his handcuffs at his back. "Maybe you feed me with the beautiful hands now, hey?"

"In my waistcoat pocket," Avila murmured. "The key. Careful!"

Pike came over, dug out the key and unlocked Tamargo's cuffs, then told him to put his hands in front. As the manacles were snapped back on, Tamargo watched the woman's face, using his eyes to make her aware of him. He saw her head lift, faint color tinge her face, and was amused.

Roxanne handed him the plate and went back to sit by the fire. As he ate, Tamargo continued to watch her, enjoying her discomfort. Her hair glowed in the coppery light; he wondered what glowed under that cool white skin. The soiled jacket was tailored boldly and deftly, outlining her

131

shoulders, her arms; it sculptured two deep breasts. Hand-sized, ripely thrusting, they made him think of Celestina . . . Celestina, the melon-bosomed slut who had betrayed him.

She had drawn him into her web so very neatly before springing the trap. The details were still muddy in his brain, since he'd been *borracho* nearly all the time he was with her. Now it was very clear what she'd had in mind all along.

When he had first come to the Salazar camp, his presence had made the people uneasy. Mexicans everywhere knew his reputation as a *pistolero* and troublemaker. For that same reason, though, none had disputed his presence too loudly. And so he stayed on, laying all the cantina sluts and getting *borracho* every night on bad pulque.

Then, the arrival of Celestina. She'd come with the muleskinners who carried supplies to the remote mining hamelt every two weeks. Nobody knew where she was from or why she had chosen Salazar; in view of her profession it had seemed pointless to ask. She was easily the best-looking prostitute in the place, and she had taken a prompt interest in Tamargo. After that it had been all Celestina, every night and most of every day.

Sometime, he couldn't recall exactly when, she had first broached the notion of robbing the payroll safe at the mine office. It had seemed a good idea. The safe held plenty of cash just before payday, and Celestina had used her charms, her wiles and her body on one of the company officials, extracting from him, bit by bit, all the information Tamargo needed. When the payroll money arrived from the East, how it was guarded, who worked in the office, and what hours they kept. Meantime Cayetano had studied the layout of the camp and the quickest way out. Celestina would wait for him in the hills.

On a quiet Saturday afternoon, Tamargo had strolled into the mine office, his face masked by black silk, and put a gun on the lone clerk. The moment he did, he was covered from all the doors and windows by a half-dozen guns. Celestina was on hand to spit in his face and tell him why she had given him away to Avila: she was the sister of that Nogales whore he had choked to death a year before, escaping trial for lack of evidence.

Cayetano opened and closed his sinewy hands, thinking how pleasant it would be to fix them around Celestina's smooth olive neck. He had two goals. Escape; and wringing the head of that treacherous little *puta* from her shoulders.

He could easily add a third goal. His eyes burned deeply on Roxanne Harris. Ah — to enjoy his freedom with this one. All that ripe Amazonian beauty. Those eyes of exotic jade. The hair that smoothly flamed. And her breasts: they were like swelling fruits that only waited the fingers to pluck them. *Dios!* Such a woman should be savored like a rare wine. As much as freedom, there should be time. All the time in the world. . . .

Time. How much could he count on? Another day, another night? There were the Apaches. And steel handcuffs: he strained his wrists apart till the shackles dug deep; a shudder ran through him.

Be patient, he told himself. Your chance will come.

That damned Mexican, the Duchess thought bitterly. Or Spaniard or whatever he was. She felt his eyes holding on her diamond-hard, brilliant with challenge. Roxanne was aware of a hot tightness in her throat . . . just as Tamargo was aware of the effect his look had on her. He was the kind who'd have a sixth sense about women. Why did it always have to be this way? Why did she always have to encounter men who saw

134

through her like glass? And why did they all have to be bastards?

And she couldn't blame them, either. Not really. She had come from a good family, the best of upbringings — it seemed a long time ago — and her own uncontrollable nature had led her from one reckless adventure to the next.

Suddenly she felt sick of it all. Herself and her troubles. The human tensions around her. The smell of her own sweat, the grit and filth that ingrained her clothing and chafed her flesh. This whole damned country and the dust and the sticky frying heat. Give it back to the Apaches as they should and she wouldn't be in this miserable situation.

She didn't often surrender to self-pity, and the feeling faded in a moment. But she still felt irritable and badly used, and the sobbing of that damned girl was eating at her nerves. Wasn't she good for anything but lying in a heap and whimpering? For a few minutes, anyway, it would be nice to escape that, and Tamargo's mocking stare.

Picking up her carpetbag, Roxanne walked to the end of the upper arroyo. It was tightly hemmed by the towering rocks, a sandy space between the boulders and the small stone-cradled pool on this end. Brush grew thickly around it, crowding to the pool's edge. The place was nicely secluded, hidden from the men below.

Quickly she shed her jacket, blouse and skirt. She peeled off her shoes and stockings, her camisole and drawers, then undid the pins of her coif and let the redgold hair tumble down to her shoulders. She dug a sliver of yellow soap out of her bag and wormed through the brush and crouched on the tank's stone rim. Gripping its edge, she lowered herself into the waist-deep water. Its surface was unpleasantly warm, like a tepid jelly; the deeper water was cool, the lava bottom smoothly cold under her feet.

She sluiced handfuls of water over her head and body. She flung her wet hair back, arching her body pleasurably. It was still a body to be proud of: long hard legs, sculptured thighs and calves, a flat-bellied waist a man could still span two-handed; high full breasts that were conical and coral-pointed, marble-white skin that took on a healthy glow as she scrubbed it. The body that had betrayed her so often, that she still took a perverse rebellious pride in keeping lean and strong and youthful.

You never learn, she thought. It's what led you into all the trouble, and you never learn.

You never will.

She climbed from the pool, shivering a little, and picked up her skirt and jacket, eying them with distaste. Maybe it was foolishness under the circumstances, but damned if she was getting back into these dirt-caked and seam-burst rags. She got her only change of clothes out of the bag: a dark skirt and crumpled, worn blouse, a fresh camisole and stockings.

She was fully dressed, buttoning the blouse, when she heard steps coming through the brush. She didn't hurry about fastening the last buttons. Yuma came around a rock and halted, seeing her. He had stripped his shirt off; it hung in his fist. His face didn't change, but she sensed his embarrassment.

Roxanne seated herself on the sand and began combing her damp hair. She grinned at him. "Don't mind us girls."

After a moment, a little stiff-backed, he walked to the pool's edge and kneeled down, scooping water over his head. The muscles moved like quicksilver under his smoky skin. His wet hair shone like a horse chestnut. Oh damn, she thought. Why does he have to . . . right now? Again her throat felt tight; a hotness ran tingling to the points of her breasts. This half-breed gave a tug to her whole being, in a way she'd never known. She'd felt it from the first and had tried to deny it. She still couldn't quite believe it.

He stood up, looking self-consciously down as he shook out his shirt and shrugged it over his head and shoulders.

"Sorry."

"Don't get overwrought, for heaven's sake." She patted the ground. "Sit down a moment."

He hunkered down as an Indian would, resting elbows on knees. Each of his wrists, she noticed, was circled by old ridges of scar tissue. His hands were smaller than most men's, but they were square, blunt-fingered; they looked unusually strong. A shiver ran down her back. She was a sucker for hands. Men's hands, and the infinite caprice of which they were capable if a man knew how to use them.

He was toying with a flat splinter of wood that hung from a leather thong on his neck.

"What's that thing?"

"A *tzi-daltai.*"

"Huh? Is that something Apache?"

"It's an amulet." He said it slowly, as if with reluctance. "Personal medicine."

"You believe in that?"

"Some, likely. I was raised on it." He held

it out on his palm. She saw that it was old and dark-worn, polished from handling. It had been roughly whittled in the shape of an armless short-legged man, zigzag lines carved on the chest. "That's *ittindi* — lightning." He turned the fetish over; twin crosses were cut in the back. "These mean *intchi-dijin,* the black wind."

"What's it supposed to do?"

"Protect you from all harm."

"Ha. I could use something like that."

"You have to work to make it good. I was fourteen. I climbed a straight-up cliff and sat on a mountain for two days. Froze all night and fried all day. And fasted. Then I cut a pine branch and made this and threw *hoddentin* to the winds. I went down to the rancheria and had the *izze-nantan* pronounce a blessing. He's the man of medicine."

"Guess nothing turns out for much if you don't sweat at it some." She worried her underlip between her teeth. "It never works the easy way, does it?"

He turned those odd off-color eyes on her. "When did your husband leave you?"

The question surprised her. She wanted to laugh it off and couldn't — quite. "When I was twenty-three. Eight years ago. Do I look thirty-one to you? Never mind. Unfair question. I'm — let's see . . . five years older than you."

"Six."

"All right, don't be gallant. Stand up once." They both stood, and she faced him eye to eye. "Funny. I'm as tall as you and I'm six years older."

"You couldn't be my ma," Yuma observed dryly. "But what of it?"

"Don't know. I have the curiousest damned feeling. As if I'm looking *up* to you."

"How does it feel?"

"I'm not sure yet." The attempted lightness didn't come off; she bit hard at her lip. "I'm envious, damn it. You've hit every bump in the road. Yet you *care* about things. I have a feeling that's why life works for you."

"I got a feeling too. You care, all right."

She smiled twistedly. "I'm female and curious, that's all. About you . . . I admit it." She took his hand in hers and ran a finger around his scarred wrist. "That, for instance. How'd you get it?"

"Snake Pit at Yuma. They chain you to the floor. Ankles too."

"My God . . . what for?"

"White man's justice. I was in the wrong place at the wrong time. A man lifted same cattle and drove 'em off and later I happened to be camped where his trail crossed when a posse came up. They didn't see no cattle, but it figured I had to be an accomplice anyway."

"Why, for God's sake?"

"Same reason I got tried and sentenced on no evidence. The sheriff and judge faced elections and an arrest and conviction would look good. Had to be someone lowdown enough nobody would complain. Wasn't no other strange breeds around to frame up." His tone was matter-of-fact, dead to bitterness. "I served my two years and took the name of the place to remember it by. Yuma. I was seventeen and eighteen those years. White man's justice."

"I don't . . ." She let go of his hand, shaking her head. "It doesn't make sense."

"What don't?"

"That you're here . . . trying to keep a passel of whites alive."

"Maybe there's a few worth saving. And one good black man."

"Even so. What do you owe any of us? Not a damned thing, mister. Alone, you could break out . . . make a good try anyway."

"All right," he said slowly. "There's another reason. I got a brother. A full-blood. I saved his life once. He hates my guts."

"For saving his life?"

"You'd have to know him. He's took it out on a lot of people. Once he killed some friends of mine. He's killed a lot of others. Maybe he'll kill a few here. Or maybe I can stop him."

"He's out there . . . with those Apaches?"

He didn't seem to hear her. His eyes had gone hard and intent on a thought. "One bullet would stop him. The others might pull off then. They just might."

"Your . . . brother?"

"Cipriano."

"Oh." Her voice caught. "You didn't have to tell. . . ."

Brush crunched under someone's foot. Yuma came pivoting around fast. Sarge stepped into sight around the rock that had hidden him. He stood not twenty feet away, his tough meaty face grinning.

"Christ," he said. "That's really something, ain't it?"

CHAPTER NINE

Sarge had eased up on the two of them for one purpose: to eavesdrop. And what he'd heard was enough to balloon his festering suspicions of Yuma into a full-blown certainty. Tramping back to the lowest part of

142

the arroyo, he yelled that he had something to tell all of them.

Yuma stood by while Sarge told what he'd heard. Watching their faces, he knew it wasn't good. Even Crim Purdy and John Twill looked worried. A cold anger washed through him: what did they want from him anyway?

Purdy turned a blue-splintered look on him. "What about it, Pike?"

"That's how it is. I'm a son of Cuchillo . . . Cipriano's my half-brother."

"I'd say," Purdy said slowly, "that you sort of took us in, boy."

"I didn't take you into a damned thing." Yuma blunted the edge on his words by keeping them soft. "I pulled you out of something, remember? You'd be dead back there, all of you, hours ago. Or maybe alive, staked on an anthill. Or strung upside down over slow fires with your brains roasted."

"Bullshit!" Sarge almost shouted. "We'd stayed in the open, we wouldn't be in this goddam trap! He brung us here to set us up for Cipriano!"

"Use your head!" Roxanne said impatiently. "Does that make any kind of sense? He did his best to cover our trail. He led us to water. He shot two of those bucks."

Sarge jabbed a calloused finger at her.

"Thing is, Duchess, he knowed Cipriano was coming. He *knowed,* by God! I had a feeling about that." He wheeled toward Yuma. "You knowed it, didn't you? Answer up! . . . I'll kick your ugly siwash face in, by Christ!"

"I knew it," Yuma said.

"There! Jesus, what more you people need?"

Purdy scratched his chin; studying Yuma narrowly. "You ain't denying it?"

"No reason to. I never lied to you."

"Shit!" Sarge said. "You set us up for them bastards. Goddam your gall —"

His hand whipped around to the flap of his service holster. Yuma braced, his fingers curving. Someone swiftly levered a Winchester. It was Severn off to his right, holding the barrel leveled at his ribs. His smile was like glazed ice.

"Why don't you, Mr. Pike?"

Purdy stepped between Sarge and Yuma, moving his own rifle in a warning gesture. "You keep your finger offen that trigger," he told Severn. "Sarge, you cool your mouth now. We got to get the straight of this."

"You won't get no straight from this goddam siwash. Christ, Mr. Purdy."

"We'll hear his side."

Yuma said softly, stubbornly: "I never lied

to you."

"Maybe not, boy. But you sure-hell omitted a thing or two."

"When I met up with your bunch, you all give me a fishy eye. Mulrooney was hellfire to have my scalp then. Suppose I'd plainout told you I was kin to Cipriano?"

"By now he's proved that doesn't mean anything," Roxanne put in sharply. "For heaven's sake, Crim!"

"All right, Duchess, all right. Said I'd hear his side, didn't I? There's just a couple things stick in my craw. Damn hard to feature just running by pure accident into a breed who turns out to be Cipriano's brother. And a sight harder to fancy any kin of that 'pache siding the white-eyes against him."

"It wasn't no accident," Yuma said flatly. "I was looking for Cipriano before I took the girl away from them four."

"Why?"

"I had a bullet with his name on it."

Severn laughed. "Oh, of course. Why else?"

"Leave him tell it," Purdy said.

Yuma told them what he'd told Roxanne, studying their faces as he talked. Twill had a black man's instinct for masking his feelings around white, but Yuma felt his sympathy glimmer through. Purdy seemed half-convinced. For Sarge and Severn and the Slaughter girl, suspicion had already hardened into conviction; nothing he could say would shake their belief: he was the enemy.

Purdy scrubbed a palm over his rusty whiskers. "Maybe it's reasonable . . . but goddammit all, Pike."

"I have a suggestion," said Severn in an idle, amused tone. "What d'you all say to another vote?"

Roxanne said: "On what?"

"Why, on whether to shoot the fellow now or save him for the authorities."

"We won't none of us get out of here alive," Sarge growled. "But this son of a bitch will if we don't finish him."

"A sterling thought," Severn said. "One I heartily second."

"Mister, you're talking about a man's life!" Roxanne said hotly. "Who d'you think you are? God?"

"My dear Duchess, I'm trying to proceed along democratic lines. If you disagree, cast your voice accordingly. It's understood, of course, that if we keep the fellow alive, we'll have to tie him up . . . unless somebody wants the onerous task of watching him day and night. It's like taking out insurance."

"Kill him," Beth Ann said softly. "Kill him!"

Roxanne looked at her. "You miserable tramp," she said quietly. "The man saved your skin."

Severn smoothed a finger along his mustache, smiling. "Of course there's one other option. We can send him out to the Apaches. If they kill him, we'll know he was telling the truth, won't we?"

"All right," Purdy said wearily. "We'll tie him up. I guess there ain't no other answer." His glance raked across Sarge, Severn, the girl. "There ain't going to be no killing."

Yuma was still braced, ready, watching all of them now.

Purdy shook his head. "Don't do it, boy. You can't take us all. Give me that gun."

Yuma let his muscles settle. "Take it."

Purdy sidled up to him in a gingerly way and lifted the pistol from its holster. After taking the Spanish dagger too, he motioned at a lava slab. "Sit down, son. Put your back to that."

Yuma sat on the ground and jammed his back against the boulder. He folded his arms, watching them from under his tipped-down hat. At the moment, angry disgust boiling in his guts, he didn't give a damn for the lot.

Sarge got a rope and cut off pieces to tie Yuma's hands and feet, jerking the knots brutally tight. The men trudged back to their positions around the arroyo. The pebbly earth was hot on Yuma's back; he rolled over a couple times till he was in the shade not far from Tamargo. The *pistolero* showed his teeth, grinning.

"Hey. *Muchacho.* That's how she go sometime, huh? Say, the *soldado,* he is right? You set up these gringos for your brother, huh?"

"The hell with you," Yuma said. He tested the ropes; they only dug deeper. His blood was almost cut off as it was.

Roxanne came up and knelt beside him.

"Those fools," she said bitterly. "Their brains must be scrambled. Pike, I'm really sorry."

"They're scared, I reckon."

"It's more than that, and you know it." Her voice sank to a whisper. "Listen . . . you said you could get out of here, alone. Even on foot you'd stand some sort of a chance."

"Maybe. I ain't about to get out, though."

"I feel to blame." Her tongue touched her lips. "If you hadn't told me . . . why did you?"

"I don't know."

"I think I do. You wanted to trust someone . . . you had to. You can't hold it in all the time, Pike."

Her hands rested on her knees; one hand moved. He saw something hidden in a fold of her skirt glitter between her fingers. She raised the hand that held the small knife tight against her thigh, letting the knife slip down to the sand.

"If you need anything, holler." She smiled and stood up, turned and walked away.

The knife was two inches from his arm on the side away from Tamargo, who was staring after Roxanne. Yuma shifted his body: a quick twist and his body was covering the knife, its miniature hilt gouging his shoulder blade.

In a few hours it would be dark. Probably they'd mount a guard or two; the rest would sleep. A good chance he could free his hands and feet unnoticed. Then . . . maybe. Just maybe.

Darkness came. For a time all of them were too jittery for sleep; they did little talking, their voices hushed and underpitched. They kept a small fire going and took turns warming themselves by it. There had been no shot, no sign at all, from the Apaches for hours. The flamelight polished the looming rock faces that circled the arroyo. The night out beyond was a black well, forbidding and strange, another world: the night world of the desert.

Toward midnight, exhaustion and frayed nerves began taking a toll. One after another they stretched out near the fire. The men discussed a guard watch. Purdy said one guard would be enough: the Apaches would attempt nothing by night; dawn was the time to look for trouble. They all badly needed sleep, and the men would split the watch; he'd take the first one.

Yuma lay on his side, knees pulled up, and feigned sleep. He was in a position to watch all the sleepers, keeping an eye on their faint movements as they settled down, dropping off one by one. Particularly he watched Tamargo — being sure that like himself the Spaniard was faking, waiting his chance. Tamargo's feet had been tied, his hands manacled behind him again.

Just now it appeared that any notions either of them had regarding escape were pretty well checkmated. Purdy had taken up a station with his back to a lava slab; he could keep an eye on both prisoners and keep a lookout of sorts on the night.

Perhaps an hour passed while the fire ebbed to red coals.

Yuma kept culling the ordinary sounds of

night; he picked out nothing unusual. You could never be a hundred percent sure about Cipriano, but he didn't guess there'd be a night attack. Cipriano had always been a superstitious bastard, respectful of taboos. If any of his men tried a move, it wasn't likely to be on his order.

Purdy kept nodding off. His head would settle against his chest, then he'd snap awake again. The glowing pocket of firelight had narrowed, both prisoners were in partial shadow now. Yuma saw Tamargo stir faintly, and then he was sure: the big Spaniard was like a coiled spring, wakeful and alert.

Purdy got to his feet and tramped back and forth, fighting weariness. He sat down again, pulled out his watch, glanced at it, shook his head and put it away. It must be getting toward the end of his shift; he was dangerously fatigued and too stubborn not to stick it out through the last minute.

He sat bolt upright for a while, but it tired his back and he leaned against the slab again. In less than five minutes, his chin sank. He slept.

Lying on his side, Tamargo slowly bent his knees and hiked his feet backward and up till he could reach his ankle ropes with his hands. The knot was tight, but the few inches of chain between the cuffs gave his

151

long powerful fingers room to work.

Yuma stayed quiet. Tamargo's break for freedom would alert the camp; it would cut his own chances to nothing. And what other chance did he have?

Just one, he thought. Cut off Tamargo's escape, then hope for the best. But not yet . . . let the Spaniard start his move.

Tamargo rolled on his belly and then, with jackknifing twists of his legs and torso, began to inch snakelike across the sand toward the sleeping Avila. Yuma located Roxanne's knife with his fingers and writhed over on his side and hunched his own bent legs up backward. He slashed blindly at the ropes.

Tamargo, making almost no sound, reached Avila's side. A strong twisting of his body brought him up to his knees, his back to the lawman. His fingers ran lightly over Avila's chest and found the pocket of his waistcoat and slipped out the key. The cuffs chinked softly; one slid off. Then the other. Gently Tamargo laid the manacles down on the sand, then rose to his feet in a long-jointed movement.

Yuma felt the razorlike blade part one loop of his ropes. His fingers worked awkwardly at the stiff coils; he felt them fall away, freeing his legs. But Tamargo, already on his feet, was catfooting lightly across the sand toward Purdy and the slack-held rifle across Purdy's knees.

Yuma hesitated. His hands were still bound; a yell would alert Purdy. But Tamargo would be on the driver before he could fully rouse himself.

Yuma pulled his body into a tight ball and rolled up onto his haunches. Lunging to his feet, he launched himself in a bentover run at Tamargo's back. The *pistolero* heard a quick whisper of boots; he started to turn. Yuma barreled side-on into him, his head and shoulders smashing into Tamargo's ribs with a teeth-jolting impact. The two of them went sprawling.

"Purdy!" Yuma yelled, rolling swiftly away from Tamargo and onto his feet.

The Spaniard was crawling to his hands and knees, half-stunned, as Purdy got bewilderedly to his feet. "Christ!" Unsure exactly what had happened, he held the rifle trained on both men.

"He got loose," Yuma said.

The others began to stir, grumbling out of their blankets, muttering questions at each other. Purdy stared a moment longer, and then he understood. He prodded Tamargo to his feet and stood back, throwing a hard-eyed look at Yuma.

"Thanks. But you might of sung out."

"No time."

Twill kicked up the fire and threw on some more sticks. Tamargo gave Yuma a sour grin.

"That was ver' stupid, *muchacho.* If I got this sleepy man's rifle, we could of leave' together. You, me."

"Sure."

Sarge said: "What'n hell happened?"

"Let Pike tell it," Purdy said. "Go on, son."

Yuma told it. Most of it. Sarge went over and picked up the cut ropes. He saw the knife and scooped it up and gave Roxanne Harris a yellow-eyed glance.

"Wouldn't just be yours, would it, Duchess?"

"Why, Sarge — the very idea."

"Never mind," Purdy said grimly. "It don't matter. Pike stopped him. Maybe saved my life too."

"That don't prove a goddam thing," Sarge growled.

"I ain't asking, Mulrooney." Purdy pulled a clasp knife from his pocket, opened the blade, stepped over to Yuma and cut away the ropes on his wrists. "Any of you think it's worth a fight," he said then, "you fight us both."

154

CHAPTER TEN

John Twill was dreaming; he grunted and twitched in his sleep. He woke suddenly, jerking upright, washed in a cold sweat. The fire was dead, and for a bewildered moment he only sat and looked about him. Then the hard black outline of lava slabs against a paling purple sky made sense, and he remembered where he was. He fumbled in the semidark for his watch and managed to make out the time . . . five minutes to four. Almost his shift.

He rose stiffly to his feet, ran his hands over his hair and grimaced as he brushed clods of damp sand from his clothing. A wry smile touched his mouth. Years of fairly luxurious living as a house slave, then a body servant, had made him almost too fastidious. Twill's bedrock contained a self-deprecating quirk of humor that was natural to him, not bred-in: how fastidious could a darky born in a turnip field become, after all?

He picked up his rifle, glanced around at the dark forms of the sleepers, then stepped carefully and quietly around one. The sleeper moved: it was Yuma Pike, coming promptly awake at the faint sound. His eyes glimmered open, turned briefly on Twill, then closed again. The man was like an animal in his reactions, Twill reflected as he trudged up the arroyo. He possessed, Twill thought with a stab of envy, all of an animal's unthinking courage.

Maybe it was less of courage than a tempered evaluation of existence in the whole sense: an awareness of his own ant-like dimensions and the naked acceptance that some day even this fragment of consciousness must end. That it didn't much matter how or when so long as a man had lived his allotted time to the full. God, Twill thought. I do envy him. . . .

He reached the arroyo's end and climbed up the lookout rock where Severn was keeping his shift.

"My watch, sir," he said with dry courtesy.

Severn said, "About time," his tone cross-grained with irritation. He looked uncomfortable, seated on a rough bare rock. He gave his ex-body servant a long speculative stare, as if hunting for any detail to find fault with.

Twill gave a mild chuckle.

"What the devil's so funny?"

"Nothing, sir. Just thinking how terribly improper of me . . . leaving your service on such short notice."

"That's the least of your sins, John,"

Severn said coldly.

"I know. I was uppity, sir."

Even in the predawn dimness he could see a vein starting to throb in the white man's temple.

"Don't preen yourself, boy," Severn said softly. "Your kind is a mere symptom of the disease that's ravaged our homeland. A disease imported by those bastard carpetbaggers and seeded like plague in a lot of ignorant nigger brains. Niggers who've filled our legislative houses and run our system into the ground. What the war didn't destroy, your ilk finished off."

"Well, sir . . . you white massas always did know what was best for us."

"We created a system of order and beauty and dignity," Severn whispered. "Our society graced the crudities of American civilization like a rare jewel. And you black beasts and your carpetbagging friends ran it into the muck."

"Perhaps we did behave a little badly," Twill murmured. "People unaccustomed to power, kept in deliberate ignorance, often abuse sudden privilege. Look at the French Revolution. But what to say of *your* use of power? . . . All that vaunted culture, that fine structure of order and law, to support a slave regime."

157

"A requisite of higher culture. You're so damned learned . . . the greatest civilization of all, that of Greece, was reared on slavery: freeing the aristocrat minds and hands for better works."

"But it was the freemen of Athens, not her decadent aristocracy or her corrupt senators, who became her great thinkers and artisans. The free black man in America could make his contribution, too . . . given opportunity."

"Opportunity for what?" Severn's mask sloughed away; his icy contempt slashed out. "To stamp your black-ape looks on the faces of our posterity? To corrupt our purest bloodlines with the mark of the beast? I know you damn lusting buck-niggers. That's the secret crest of your aspiration, isn't it? That our daughters bear your sons' little burr-headed monsters."

Twill's hands opened and closed slowly around his rifle: he couldn't quite keep the trembling from his evenly controlled voice. "My aspiration, sir, would be to raise a son who is not such a damned fool as to covet any daughter of yours."

Severn rose to his feet, his slender frame like a ramrod. His rifle barrel was pointed down, and he began to raise it. Dryness thickened Twill's throat, but he matched the threatening move with his own rifle. Severn's eyes glittered.

"Get out of my way, Sambo," he said softly.

Twill moved slowly and warily, enough to let Severn step past him and descend the clustering rocks. He watched Severn stride with a stiff-backed rage down the arroyo, and drop down by a rock some distance from the sleepers. Severn got out a cigar, struck a match, and drew the cigar alight, puffing furiously.

Twill ignored him, gazing across the gaunt sepia range with its lead-colored veins of naked rock, cold-looking now in the chill of fading night and a mild rising current of wind. Something lightly rattled, almost making him jump. It was, he saw, only the dry pods on a spiky clump of soapweed just below him. He shivered and settled back, clutching the rifle across his knees. Be a big bad Western man, he thought bitterly. Be brave for once.

A faintness of voices reached him. He turned his head. One of the sleepers had come over to join Severn. It was the Slaughter girl.

"You mind, mister?" she murmured. "I can't sleep."

"Not at all, miss. Please . . . sit down."

"I knowed you wouldn't mind. You're a gentleman." She bunched down beside him. "I'm just so blamed scared . . . I can't help it."

"Of course you can't. You've been through a great deal. But you mustn't give up hope."

"I surely don't want to." Her voice shuddered and softly broke. "I just hate this awful country so. All I want is to get away from it."

"I don't blame you. It's no place for so pretty and fragile a creature as yourself."

The girl was silent a moment, as if awed. Then: "I tried to run away once . . . sneaked out on one of the stages. Pa caught up and took me back and larruped me something fierce."

"You mustn't despair," Severn told her gently. "You're very young — and very pretty. A whole world is waiting. . . ."

It continued pretty much in that vein. The girl's voice vehement, bitter, self-pitying. And Severn's: encouraging her confession of shallow dreams, warm with his assurances. How many times, Twill wondered, had he heard the white man go through more or less this same routine in his female conquests? Severn thought no more of carrying on intimately before a black man than he would in front of a dog or a cat. For

160

Twill, this — as much as anything — had always been the bitter calibration of his place in the white man's world.

Why? It was an eternal question in Twill's mind; an involuntary self-loathing tinged it. What's the difference between this white man and me? Physically, I could smash him with one hand. I'm his equal — perhaps his superior — in intelligence and education. I'm as well-spoken, my manners as polished. So why? I can reduce all the reasons to objective terms — historical, social, morbidly pathological. But why, God? Why?

Severn, an intense cynic who nevertheless clung to the holy rags of his past, was typical of his class. They all loved the nigger, but let any goddam nigger try to be human. Stupid? Some gentlefolk were; others must know in a corner of their minds what nonsense they hewed to. What brutality and inequity had flowed from the system where, supposedly, practically all slaveowners were loving masters and their slaves like beloved children. But none of them, Twill thought, ever suspected the deeper wasting scar that generations of dumb-brute servitude had branded on the black man's soul: the shriveling away of that vital core that made him a man. And with it, the drying-up of all courage, all resolution, all will to fight back.

There was the real, the only difference between Severn and himself.

He was going to die on this desert. Twill felt it, he knew it. And I'm afraid, he thought. My hunter and warrior ancestors of the veldts . . . they were men. What they were must be atrophied somewhere under my black skin. But I can't touch it. And I'm afraid. As little as my life is worth, I'm terrified of losing it. . . .

The voices of Severn and the girl had dropped to muted murmurs. Once she gave a bold cajoling giggle. Twill didn't even glance their way, but his nerves prickled with irritation.

A horse whickered nervously. Twill strained his eyes toward the brush-fronted corral, but couldn't tell anything. Promptly Yuma Pike was on his feet; he went across to the corral and looked inside and spoke to the horses. Afterward he tramped up the arroyo, glanced without interest at Severn and the girl as he passed them, and climbed up into the rocks beside Twill.

"How's it look out there?"

"All right, but don't suppose I could tell if it weren't." Twill smiled wryly. "Anything wrong with the horses?"

"That dead one has got 'em spooky. He'll get bloating soon. We'll pile some dirt over him." Yuma stared out at the rock field. "Getting light, Mr. Twill. That's the time to watch sharp. First light."

That's why he came up here, Twill thought. "Mr. Pike . . . do you really think we have any sort of chance?"

"So long as we stand 'em off. If they get into the arroyo, we're done for. So far everyone's holding up good, pulling his share. Everyone but Slaughter's girl."

"You can hardly cite me as a model of fortitude."

"You done all right."

Twill looked at the rifle in his hands as if he weren't quite sure why it was there. "I'm frightened, Mr. Pike . . . plain gut-deep scared. I know I'll funk out if they attack."

"You won't. Not when it comes. You'll fight."

"You're so sure," Twill said coldly. "Why should I fight? For what? These lily-white souls?"

"For yourself. To stay alive."

"Again . . . why?" Suddenly it was boiling up to his throat like hot bile: a brass-bitter cry from the well of his lost manhood. "To play the whole man here . . . stay alive so I can return to being a half-man? Living the mockery of freedom allowed me by the white massas? God! Give me the slavery that wasn't diluted by hypocrisy."

"I do admire your way with words, Mr. Twill," Yuma said dryly. "You really mean all that, it's like I told you before. Stand fast and fight. Man who lives one second of that whole life you talk about is a sight better off than a fella spends a lifetime hating himself for a half man."

"You've done it, haven't you? In spite of . . . the color thing. You've lived on your terms, not theirs. And managed to stay alive."

"I manage."

Twill smiled acridly. "Well, I can't, Mr. Pike. Not your way. I'm not a loner, I'm not tough and self-reliant, I'm not used to the terrible privations you take for granted. Once I knew privation . . . and I have a horror of it. My very early youth was nothing but . . . and after a year at Massa's big house, warm, comfortable, well-fed, I wouldn't have gone back for the world. Thirty years of it now, except for the interlude after the war . . . thirty years of soft living."

"Be hard going back, I reckon."

"I never will. I —"

Yuma raised his hand sharply.

"What is it?" Twill whispered.

Yuma didn't answer; his face was alert,

hard as bone. Twill ran his eyes across the rock-strewn land. It was lightening by the minute, turning from ashy beige to a dull buff. The sky was pale and the tips of the Santa Catalinas to the north were tinged a yellowish pink where the unseen sun touched them in its rising.

He heard a soft whistling call. A quail?

One moment there was nothing but a motionless landscape of brush and rock. The next, a scatter of moving forms seemed to materialize out of the ground. They came in a rush.

Yuma's rifle boomed down the silence, the heavy report almost deafening Twill. An Apache went down clutching his belly, kicking away his life. The shot brought the men in the arroyo to their feet, shaking away the dregs of sleep, grabbing for their rifles. Yuma's big gun blasted again; another Indian was slammed off his feet, falling like a broken doll.

The whites were at their posts in seconds, grilled to instant response by yesterday's blistering vigil. Twill had a dim awareness, from the long burst of gunfire at his back, that the Apaches were rushing their other flank too. The rapid-firing Winchesters shattered the dawn with a mingling stacatto crash.

There were yells. Someone screamed.

The glassy freeze of fear around Twill's brain cracked: his rifle hard against his shoulder began hammering shots. He had no consciousness of hitting anything. He saw everything through a glaze of unreality: leather-colored ghosts surging at him through the spectral light. They must not reach the rocks, he knew that much, not a one must get past him.

Yuma was down out of the rocks, running at the nearest breach as an Apache's wiry form began squirming through it. Twill saw Yuma sweep the heavy Sharps barrel up and down. He distinctly heard the sickening crush of bone and saw the Apache slump, his body wedging between the slabs.

All was confusion. Men shouting, men shooting. Somehow, Twill realized, he was in the thick of it and the feral-bull bellowing that filled his ears came from his own throat. Suddenly a squat warrior had cleared the rocks with a leap and was coming at him and he was pointing the Winchester and feeling the scrape of metal as it jammed clear in the pit of his guts.

The buck was on him, steel flashing in his lifted fist. Twill grappled him and fell with him, smelling the grease-and-woodsmoke stink of him, rolling over and over and gripping with both hands the fist holding the knife. They stopped rolling and he was on top, the buck's blue-and-vermilion-streaked face glaring into his inches away.

The Apache's violent heave flung him partly off and Twill involuntarily let go with one hand. He felt the other slipping from its hold. He scrambled wildly away from his adversary; he plunged across the sand on his hands and knees toward a glittering object. It lay by one limp hand of the buck Yuma had shot between the rocks. A hatchet.

He closed his hand over the handle and felt the shock of sticky warmth coating it. In one split measuring instant the sensation shocked him to total reality. Floundering around on his knees, he saw the buck coming at him, face darkly contorted, knife whipping high again.

Twill threw the hatchet. Did it with an agonizing clarity of intent. Saw it loop once in its flight and heard it meet flesh and bone with the moist meaty thunk of a butcher's cleaver. The Apache's legs melted and he fell like a stone, sprawling and turning. He stopped in a dusty lump. The hatchet was sunk fast in his skull, the handle angling up grotesquely.

Twill rose and shook himself and looked

around. The Apaches were in retreat. A little more scattered shooting: then they were gone, driven off. It had happened so quickly, and it was already over. Only the one he'd killed had gotten past the line of defense. He saw that Yuma Pike was watching him and found it somehow strange that Massa Severn was too.

Twill's stomach roiled. He looked at the sticky darkness on his palm and closed his fist on it. Lord God. A singing red-tinged brightness seared his brain. Lord . . . this is how it is. If I can fight like a man, I can die like a man.

Abruptly he dropped to his hands and knees and vomited up every particle in his belly. This time it was, in a way, a purging.

CHAPTER ELEVEN

There was a casualty. Sarge Mulrooney. A bullet had hit him in the head, killing him instantly.

A serious blow to their fighting strength, for the feisty veteran had been a dead shot with the big service .45 that had dropped two Apaches in the attack. Purdy had killed or badly wounded a third. The three bodies were gone, carried off by the Apaches in their retreat. Dark patches marked where they had fallen: otherwise the simmering landscape was empty again, and the sun was high.

Using only their hands, the men had finished excavating a broad trench to hold Sarge and the two Apaches killed by Yuma and Twill. When they had filled it and mounded the dirt over it, they sprawled in the shade and soaked in their own sweat, dumb, blank-eyed, exhausted. Roxanne Harris took the watch while they rested, and Yuma kept doggedly on his feet. The dead horse had to be covered up, the live animals tended to.

He watered the horses at the lowest tank, noting that the sizzling heat and their combined thirsts had caused the water level to drop noticeably in twenty-four hours. The horses had already cropped off most of the mesquite leaves and all the galleta grass. The plants Yuma had improvised as food for his companions were almost exhausted; the surviving quail refused to fall for his snares.

The water wouldn't last forever; the food situation was already desperate. Yuma inspected the bow and quiver of arrows that had belonged to the Apache he'd brained. It was a weapon he knew well, it would kill silently, and bighorn had watered at these tanks. They had to be nearby . . . probably in the high ridges. A species different from the mountain bighorns who ranged farther north, they made fine eating.

"Come dark," he told the others, "I'll try to sneak out and get us a sheep."

"That," said Severn, "would be the last we'll see of you."

"Reckon I'll be back." The Southerner's empty venom no longer touched him. "They'd run me down by daylight."

"Maybe we all better go," Purdy said. "Try with the horses. Way things are, we ain't got a lot to lose."

"There's still too many of us," Yuma said. "Supposing three made it out on horses . . . ones who stayed wouldn't hold out an hour. Cipriano lost five in that rush. Good chance he won't try another. He can't afford them kind of losses. Different if the odds were cut, though."

"I have a thought." Severn had gotten to his feet. He spoke so crisply that everyone looked at him. "Suppose you take a horse and try to break out, Pike. If it's you he really wants, he might drop everything else."

"Two things wrong with that," Yuma said. "He can't give up on you if he wants. Not and hold his men. Too many of 'em have died here. That's hitting 'em where their pride's deepest. They'll take a sight more care now, but they won't quit while a one of you's left alive."

Severn's grin was cold and bone-gaunt, a mere twitching of lips off his teeth. "And the other thing? But I can guess."

"Other thing is, I ain't in a mood for suicide. Could come to that, breaking out of here horseback."

"Then I'll take the chance." Severn's hand moved in a tight blur and his pistol was sweeping out and up; he thumbed back the hammer. "And this time, my dear breed, I'm not asking. I'm going."

Cayetano Tamargo gave a harsh croak of a laugh. "The bay, gentleman. He's still yours."

"I'll take him. Bring him out here, Purdy."

Purdy got up slowly. "You best think some harder on that, mister. Pike's right."

"The devil with Pike. By his own word, the Apaches won't give up on us. All right. If they don't attack, they can outlast us. What do we do, squat and fry in this damned hole till we're too weak to move?"

"Water'll hold out a while yet," Yuma said. "I get us a sheep, we'll have food to spare. Point is, we buy ourselves more time."

"Time for what? I've had enough of your stoical red-skin patience. It's a mask for your stupid inadequacy. The bay — get him, Purdy. Saddle him."

Purdy motioned upward with a calloused palm, a hopeless gesture, then tramped over to the horse enclosure and pulled the brush away from the entrance. Severn stood where he could see them all, but his glinting stare never left Yuma. He'd like the excuse, Yuma thought.

Twill flexed his long legs and rose.

"What the devil are you about?"

"Just stretching my legs, sir."

"Stand still, damn you."

Purdy led out the saddled bay and handed Severn the reins. The animal snuffled and tossed his head, the muscles rolling under his glossy coat. He had a deep chest, powerful shoulders, long clean legs: he would carry a man far and fast. In the open, Yuma thought. But not through those rocks at a run, his rider a clear target.

Severn moved warily against the bay's flank, put a toe in the stirrup and swung up, keeping the gun trained. He quartered the animal around with a born horseman's touch.

"I'll bid you goodbye but not for long. I'll be back with help . . . in two days at the latest."

"Ho," Tamargo chuckled. "I don't think

you fetch much help from hell."

Yuma moved, not quickly. He walked in toward the bay's right flank, only stopping when Severn said sharply: "That's far enough!"

"Better hold off. Man's dead for a long time."

"Your desert-rat truisms do sparkle, Pike. Stand aside."

Yuma stepped back a little, but also moved a little farther toward Severn's rear, forcing his attention farther around.

"Pike, don't move again —"

Severn's attention was off Twill in that moment and Yuma hoped it would be enough and that Twill, on Severn's other flank, wouldn't hesitate. He didn't. The big Negro took three long steps and then leaped as Severn's head pivoted back.

Twill grabbed him by the arm and waist and Severn slashed savagely down at his head with the pistol. Twill twisted, grunted as the barrel slammed across his neck, then dragged Severn from the saddle. Handling the Southerner like a baby, he took the pistol from him, lifting the struggling man off his feet, dumping him to the ground in a dusty sprawl.

Severn got up, and wiped his bleeding nose on his sleeve. "I'll cut your guts out for that. Sambo."

"Well, sir. You won't need a gun for that."

Twill smiled and shoved the pistol into the waistband of his trousers.

All day an angry sun poured into the arroyo. Hours dragged past. Tony Avila's condition worsened. He tossed in a furnace of deepening fever, babbling in border Spanish to a woman named Marguerite. His wife, Yuma supposed. Roxanne, sacrificing her last petticoat, changed his blood-soaked bandages for the third time. But Avila's delirious thrashings kept his wound pumping; it was useless trying to hold him down. They had no drugs to quiet him, and without a doctor's care Yuma was sure he wouldn't last another day.

The landscape baked in yellow silence. Somewhere in that dazzling desolation, the Apaches waited. And gave no sign. The people in the arroyo lay sprawled in the hot shade and boiled in the mire of their grimy sweat, and hardly talked at all.

Most of the time it was Yuma who kept the lookout. Even his flesh felt hammered by the scorching sun, but heredity and training kept his senses tight and alert. He watched his companions closely, reedy for any of them to crack under the combination of heat and sheer nervous strain. But they seemed more drained and apathetic than anything. Even the Slaughter girl had quieted down. Only John Twill, who'd found the measure of his courage, dredged up a triumphant vitality; several times he relieved Yuma on watch.

Sunset blazed. Bloodgold streamers of it ran together along the desert surface and soaked into the cooling earth. Blessed coolness. Really a relative reduction of the heat, but its loosening clutch brought relief. Twilight tarnished the sky; a small breeze feathered the drooping mesquite leaves. Slacked in his lookout perch, Yuma thought a lot about Cipriano.

One bullet, he thought. But you had to get him in your sights first. And if he did kill Cipriano, would the others pull off? The death of a leader could do it — but a lot of Apache blood had been shed here, and the price of Apache blood came high.

Think about getting that sheep tonight, he thought. Food. That was a sure thing — they needed food. On every other count, he had to proceed with care. Being responsible for a bunch of people was new to him; he faced a lot of choices. One badly chosen course of action and it would be all up with them.

Still he had to decide on something definite. And soon.

Someone was coming up the arroyo in the fading light. It was Roxanne Harris, carrying her carpetbag. She halted momentarily below his perch, turning her head to look at him. She didn't speak. Smiling a little, she walked on and was gone out of sight amid the tangle of brush and boulders that flanked the highest pool.

He stared out at the darkening desert. The restless twilight cut at him. He tried to think ahead. A soft rustle of water reached his ears. The taut rush of impulse filled him and he quit thinking about anything else. Dropping off the rock, he rounded the screening rocks and thickets and stood in the sandy space where he and Roxanne had talked before, alone.

She sat on a flat rock close by the tank, shoes and stockings off, skirt bunched up on her thighs, washing her long white legs. Her hair was loosened, falling around her shoulders; coppery twilight raced across it as she turned her head.

"Hello," she said, and stood up unhurriedly. Even in this light her eyes were vivid, like green flowing sparks.

"Pike . . . you're going out soon?"

"When it's full dark."

"Be careful. Please." Her lips hardly moved. "I didn't come to tell you that. I didn't come to wash, either."

The seep of twilight toward dusk wove a gray loom around them and the world narrowed to this secluded patch of sand. He looked at her, thinking of the differences that separated them and the hot magnetism that refused to admit it.

"Before," she murmured, "when there was a need, we talked. But there are other needs too. That's why I'm here. Why you're here."

They were standing close, facing each other. She moved — or he did. They came together suddenly. The firm thrusting breasts drove against his chest, the generous mouth twisted to his in a hungry crush, her tongue plunging and flickering, her fingers curving into his back. The minutes surged by: fierce, wordless, eloquent without words.

"This is crazy —" he managed to say.

She tore her mouth away and threw back her head. Her hair rippled, a russet mass. "Why? Why is it ever crazy, if you want to?"

"It's no time to. . . ."

"Time is what you're wasting, my friend. Mine — and yours too."

His mouth hammered into the wide soft lips. The brutal kiss resumed, her curves molding savagely to him. She moaned, writing against him in an agony of desire. They moved sideways, they tumbled together in the sand and never knew they fell. Among the high crumple of her skirts, her legs tangled frenziedly with his.

Anybody cocking his ear hard enough in the muffling dusk would have picked out noises that separated themselves from other sounds of night and told a story of their own. But nobody was listening. . . .

It was midnight when Yuma left the arroyo. Leaving Purdy up on lookout post, Twill and Severn on guard at each flank, he slipped out through a split of space between two boulders. He went under the brush like a snake, belly to the ground, inching along by twisting his hips and digging in his elbows. The buckskin quiver and mesquite bow were thonged to his back. The bow ends threatening to snag in the branches continually hampered his movements, but he'd done this before; he barely disturbed a twig as he went through.

The big danger was running into a positioned Apache somewhere in this jungle of brush-riddled rock. There'd be an outcry and he'd be lucky to make it back if he survived the encounter. He stopped every few yards and waited a full moment, sorting out the nocturnal sounds. The darkness was a drawback as well as a cover: he couldn't tell much by sight. A wedge of pale moon hung like a clot of cheese above the obsidian rim of desert, throwing only a gaunt dim sheen over the rocks.

At the end of a half hour, he was hardly fifty yards from the arroyo. No way of telling how close in and how far out the Apaches had stationed themselves, but he was sure they were at widely scattered points all around. Superstitious as hell, wary of losing their souls in the dark, few of them were likely to be roaming about.

Once, quiet and listening, he caught a padded hint of movement. Off right of him, a man's dark form flitted ghostlike down a rocky aisle; it vanished again. Yuma waited almost five minutes before he inched onward.

In another few minutes he heard a shuffling of horses. He was close to where the Apaches had their remuda bunched, he knew then. It meant checking the wind and making a painstaking detour so they wouldn't pick up his scent.

An hour went by. By then he was far beyond the arroyo, back on his feet, moving bent over through the broken lanes of brush under a corrugation of long bluffs. He was sure he was a fair distance outside the Apache lines, and he put all his attention on the hunt.

Faintly, the sounds of an animal cropping grass reached him. Somewhere off skyline, it was invisible to him. He halted, placed the sound carefully, and made sure of the wind. The strung bow was already in his hand; he eased an arrow from his quiver and nocked it. Now he moved again, but even more cautiously, keeping crouched and widely circling a smoke tree that partly obscured his vision. Once clear of it, he could see the whole undulating crest of the bluff.

Suddenly the grazing noises ceased. Yuma froze. Any sound might stampede the animal, and he'd be lucky to get this near another. He waited, his nerves tingling. He counted on the bighorn sooner or later moving from the spot and skylining himself. Patience and stealth were the primitive hunter's allies; though he hadn't hunted this way since boyhood, he fell easily into the old mental habits: wait, stay ready.

Almost imperceptibly, brush quivered somewhere at his back. At once his senses were geared to that fact. It might be a small animal; it might be anything. He listened a long time, keeping only half his attention on the bighorn. It had resumed grazing. There was a shadowy chance some Apache had heard him earlier and was stalking him. He didn't think so; if he'd really been spotted, there should have been an alarm raised. Unless the enemy wanted to score a personal coup. . . .

Uppermost was his fear that the quarry would bolt. But it grazed casually along the foot of the bluff, chomping grass, its hoofs clicking casually over the rocks.

After a time it quit grazing and shifted away in a definite direction, ranging upward along the flank of the low bluff. Yuma straightened from his crouched position, letting pressure off his cramped legs, and he was ready when the bighorn appeared suddenly in a shallow cleft at the crest. It came around sideways, pausing, silhouetting a massive curve of horns. Yuma drew the bowstring, sighting along the shaft.

In that second there was another shred of sound behind him, jarring him to a split-instant decision: shoot now or wheel to confront the possible enemy at his back.

He sent the arrow whumping home: he knew with a hunter's prompt instinct that the quartz arrowhead had sunk hard and deep behind the shoulder. The bighorn sprang a yard, it sank, it rolled hard and made a bony strike of horns on rock.

Yuma fell back to a crouch, half-turning, another arrow already fixed to his bow. His eyes furiously ferreted the masses of brush. It might still be an animal back there, but he was less sure. It was too easy to read something positive into a casual sound: imagination, he thought. Fancy was an invitation to panic.

He still wasn't sure. But he had his kill: he couldn't abandon it on a half-chance of being discovered. He backed off till he felt the slope rise under his feet, then wheeled and went up the bluff face at a lope. The bighorn had fallen between two rocks, its legs angling up, moonlight silvering the splash of white on its underside. Keeping his body as low as possible, Yuma dragged the carcass free and, working by feel, bent swiftly to the job of gutting and skinning. He had butchered it out and was starting to wrap the saddle and hindquarters in the hide when he heard the noise again.

This time it was something he could pin down: a stealthy but definite sound of someone making for the foot of the bluff. Yuma slid up to the angle of a giant rock and crouched low. He saw movement. The man was coming straight on, quietly but making no particular effort at concealment.

He glided up the slope, working around the gigantic rubble. Yuma waited, the knife in his hand still slick and warm from the skinning, wondering what it meant. Was the fellow just a damned fool . . . or what?

The Apache came around the block-shaped boulder, pivoting swiftly as Yuma sprang at him. Yuma caught a wiry wrist and felt his own knife arm grabbed and then the two of them went down in the rocks. He came atop his adversary, then heard the warning hiss:

"Gian-nah-tah!"

Yuma had his knife poised over the man's head and was straining it down with all his weight against the other's hold. Instantly he slacked up and pulled back, then climbed to his feet.

"Es-ki-min-zin," he said.

His uncle got up: tall, wire-muscled, his face barred with pale paint. "I think you've forgotten a few things, Gian-nah-tah. Maybe I didn't teach so well."

Yuma smiled. "Maybe you taught too well. I picked you up below."

"Good. But I saw you long before."

"And followed me. You could have been shot."

Es-ki-min-zin dropped to his haunches and Yuma hunkered down facing him.

183

"I could dodge your foolish arrows," Es-ki-min-zin said, and he was smiling too. "You were always bad with the bow."

"You babble like an old woman." Yuma pointed at the sheep. "It was a good kill."

"A child with a bent stick could do as well." Es-ki-min-zin reached a long arm and slapped him on the knee. "I joke. I took a chance. I knew you would not fire a gun."

Yuma peered at the grim lined face of the warrior who had been his friend and his mentor. "Did you know it was me?"

"Who else among those *pin-da lik-o-yee* would go past the *Shis-in-day* like a snake?" Es-ki-min-zin scooped up a handful of gravel and juggled it in his palm. "Maybe I am the foolish one. I wanted to talk."

"What is there to say?"

"I don't know. You are with the white-eyes."

"It is the thing between Tloh-ka and me."

"This I know." Es-ki-min-zin let the gravel trickle out between his fingers. "But you are more Apache than white."

"It is equal."

"You are more Apache. I saw to that long ago." Es-ki-min-zin laughed quietly. "That's why you fight us well."

Yuma grinned. It was a grain of humor even he found weird. He had broken the blood bond; he had killed Apaches. Killed without rancor or hatred, yet he had killed. And only an Apache would laugh and understand. His feud with Cipriano was explanation enough.

They were silent a moment. A horned owl gave a fluttering call in the night. Es-ki-min-zin looked up, around him, at the ground again. "Sometimes my eyes are black and I think it is all bad. But life is good; it is good to live. Still we must go to war. We are men."

"You never liked it."

"What does it matter what I like? When I was young, I thought too much and spoke my thoughts. When they called me a woman, I went on every war trail."

"But at the fires you still spoke. For peace."

"There is peace sometimes. But I am one voice." Es-ki-min-zin sounded very dry. "Cuchillo never heard my counsel till the white-eyes' whiskey spoiled his belly. Now he worries for Tloh-ka; he sent me with him, hoping I could bend his ways."

"Who talks to Cipriano?"

"And is heard? No man." The aging warrior was silent a moment. "How many white-eyes are left?"

"Enough. We will outlast you."

"You cannot have so much to eat. Your

water won't last. What then?"

"Then the white-eyes from Tubac will come."

"They will come, but you will all be dead."

"We will see."

Es-kin-min-zin's brows quivered upward. "Listen, Gian-nah-tah. Leave them. Fight Tloh-ka another time — another way. Last time we almost overran you. What of next time?"

"Cipriano will not attack again. He lost too many."

"He will wait, but the others won't. They are dishonored; they are angry. Sus-to burns to kill you because your bullet broke the bone of his leg. It will heal crookedly. He whips the others with words."

"I cannot leave. It is the thing with Cipriano."

A stubborn silence ran between them.

"I would say this," Es-ki-min-zin said finally. "Because we have been close, because you're of my blood, I would say it. Maybe we will both die here. It's in the hand of U-sen." He paused. "If we meet again, I will try to kill you."

"Still it will be as it was with us."

"Enju," murmured Es-ki-min-zin. "That is what I would say." His hand went out in the white man's way; Yuma took it. "Maybe I

186

will kill you or you will kill me. Still it will be as it was. . . ."

Chapter Twelve

Returning to the arroyo took even longer. He had to slither in complete silence through the brushy tangles, the hide-wrapped chunks lashed to his back. He was suddenly, bitterly tired, and some of his edge was gone. Every pebble seemed to rasp his flesh like a spike; he had to rest often, fighting exhaustion to stay on the alert for nearby enemies, at the same time checking his bearings. Forced to stay low in the brush, he could easily lose himself.

After what seemed hours, he made out the orange seep of light from the arroyo. When he was finally close to it, he was almost totally exhausted. Not wanting to be shot for an Apache, he gave the soft call of a quail which he and Purdy had agreed on for a signal.

"Hear you, Pike," came Purdy's hoarse whisper from the lookout rock just a few yards above. "Come on in."

Yuma pushed through the gap. His legs were rubbery as he straightened, shed his cargo and then sank down on his heels, letting his head hang between his knees. Purdy climbed down beside him.

"All right, boy?"

"I'll live. Any trouble?"

"Not yet. Nobody's slept. Too jittery. Severn's at it again, same song as before."

Purdy picked up the bundle of meat. Yuma dredged up strength, got to his feet, and the two of them tramped down the arroyo to the fire. Severn was striding back and forth, saying, "I think you should all consider —"

He broke off, seeing Yuma. Purdy dropped the bulky and blood-streaked hide by the fire and they all looked at it. All except Roxanne: she never took her eyes off Yuma. Slowly then, she smiled.

"Mr. Severn," she said dryly, "was allowing as how you wouldn't be back."

"Seems reasonable," Yuma said.

Severn didn't comment, but his pale eyes were yellowish and glaring. He was, Yuma thought, close to the cracking point.

They carved thin slices from one of the hindquarters and quick-grilled them on sticks over the coals. They ate these half-cooked, bolting them down almost sizzling hot, scorching their fingers and tongues. Wild mutton. It was tough, greasy, faintly bitter; it seemed delicious.

With a little rest and some warm food in his belly, Yuma felt better. He went off from the others and settled on his heels and did some hard thinking.

The chances that they could withstand the strains and privations of a straight siege till the arrival of a relief party from Silverton or Tubac (God knew when) were decidedly thin. And if Es-ki-min-zin was right, their situation was a sight too serious to allow for waiting. Yuma bleakly weighed the odds against their surviving one more attack like the last. Even if their ammunition wasn't almost exhausted, he doubted they could hold the enemy off. Sarge was dead, Avila was out of it, Twill a hopelessly bad shot. Neither woman could handle a gun and he wouldn't trust Tamargo with one.

If Es-ki-min-zin had called the turn correctly and Cipriano's control of his men were slipping, an attack would certainly come. True, Cipriano would be reluctant, and not because he wouldn't willingly sacrifice warriors if he could get his half-breed brother's scalp. It was simply bad strategy. To the Apache, war was no game. Other tribes might encourage their young men to seek glory with grandiose charges on horseback and coup-counting. But the Apache fought first for survival, second for loot, and only incidentally for glory. A war chief's prestige was proportionate to the amount of damage he inflicted on an enemy at the least cost. If he lost men, he was a bad leader.

Cipriano faced a harsh dilemma. He had already lost enough men to seriously undercut his influence among the Chiricahua. If, in addition, he failed to wipe out this small party of *pin-da lik-o-yee,* his disgrace would be ineradicable. He couldn't afford to attack — and he couldn't afford not to. But his warriors' restiveness would be enough, Yuma guessed, to tip the balance. Cipriano would be forced to order a do-or-die charge on the arroyo.

When? As soon as possible. Meaning predawn, when spirits no longer roamed and the light remained poor. And that hour was close. . . .

Roxanne was checking on Avila, bending down beside him. She laid her hand against his face, then stood up, her lips pinched. She glanced at Yuma.

"Will you have a look at him?"

He went over and knelt by the still form. Avila's face was waxen, his eyes closed. Yuma raised his hand and let go; it fell stiffly.

Roxanne turned away, pressing her knuckles to her teeth. Severn got up and walked over and looked down at the dead man, his jaw knotting.

"It's finished," he said, as if to himself. "Got to get out now. . . ." He had a Winchester in his hands; he raised it till the muzzle pointed at Yuma's chest. "I'm going, Pike. There's nothing to lose. Even you can see that."

Yuma looked at the rifle. "You want out bad."

"Bad enough to pull this trigger if you try to stop me."

"Mister, please." Beth Ann Slaughter got up and stumbled over to Severn. She clung to his arm, shivering, her eyes white-edged with terror. "Take me with you. Please. Don't leave me here."

"All right. Two horses, Pike. Are they worth a fight? You'll die, I promise you."

Severn kept his eyes on Yuma. Behind him, Twill was carefully bringing up his rifle, ready to lever it. Yuma shook his head.

"Take 'em. Never mind, Mr. Twill."

"Gentleman, I think I take back the bay." Tamargo had rolled to a sitting position. "Now I want to leave too."

"Don't worry about it," Yuma said.

Tamargo clashed his manacled wrists together, holding them out. "Hey. Breed. Antonio is dead, I was his prisoner. You got no right to hold me now."

"I liked Avila," Yuma said. "I think I'll take

you in."

Tamargo slacked back, smiling whitely. *"Bastardo,"* he murmured. "Maybe I will slice your gizzard, Pike. My time will come."

"I'll wait," Yuma said. He looked at Severn and Beth Ann, his belly hot with anger. "You going?"

Severn went to the enclosure and dragged the brush away and began saddling the horses.

"Pike —" Roxanne looked pale. "Don't. You're mad now, that's all. Don't let them go."

Yuma swung on his heel and faced her. "I been fighting these two since I met 'em. I done everything a man could to keep 'em alive and what I got for it is spit on my face." His voice was low and savage. "You heard that fine Southern gentleman. I try to stop him, I'm dead. Or he's dead. Either way, it ain't worth it. It ain't worth a goddam thing."

They went out through the widest breach in the rocks, Severn on the bay, Beth Ann on Avila's pinto. No shot came. In a few seconds the darkness swallowed them. Hooves clanging on rock flung back a few flinty echoes; even these faded.

Purdy remained on lookout. The rest sat

192

on the scuffed earth by the fire and nobody said anything.

Still no shots came. Yuma wondered . . . he had returned Severn's pistol. He had the Winchester too. They wouldn't be taken without shooting.

"Maybe," Roxanne said softly.

Yuma glanced at her. He made a guess and didn't answer. His straining ears began to ache.

At last a crackle of gunfire reached them: it sounded far away. And it ended quickly.

"They were sure," Yuma said. "So they waited. Let 'em get away . . . almost."

"God," John Twill whispered. "I hope that was the end of it."

But it wasn't. The screams began. And went on. . . .

There were five of them left. And one horse. The zebra dun.

Twill sat by the fire, breaking twigs in his fingers and pitching them at the raw coals, watching them flare, break into glowing wires and crumble to filigrees of pale ash. Suddenly he looked up.

"Mr. Pike. They'll attack, won't they? At dawn?"

"I reckon."

"Can we take another attack?"

"We ain't got enough guns. Even if we did stand 'em off one more time, that's it. We're low on shells."

"And we can't count on help from Tubac very soon, can we?"

Yuma shook his head.

"Well, then. As I see it, we've nothing to lose . . . by making our move before they make theirs. We can try to break out."

"We won't make it, Mr. Twill. We'll die a sight faster, that's all."

"Perhaps not. Perhaps there's a way."

Yuma glanced at Roxanne, at Purdy; they were paying close attention. When hope turned to desperation, people would listen to anything.

"Suppose," Twill went on, "that one could create a distraction that would enable the others to slip out."

"How you propose to do that?"

Twill nodded at the zebra dun, stamping restlessly behind the brush barrier. "Suppose a man took that horse and rode him hard and fast. Say they play their little game as before . . . letting him get a ways before they stop him. But suppose, before he's gone far, he leaves the horse and ducks into the rocks and gives 'em a fight. There's your distraction."

"It'll take care of a few. The rest'll see that

nobody else busts out. Anybody did, they wouldn't get far with no horse."

"Wait." Twill hunched forward, crossing his arms on his knees. "With that distraction accomplished, suppose that another of us reaches their horses. You mentioned passing close by their remuda. . . ."

"There'll be a guard."

"Who can probably be overcome . . . and the horses run off." Twill paused. "All, that is, but the few necessary to carry our party away from here. Leaving the savages afoot, their animals scattered . . . they'd be hours catching them up."

"That's quite an idea," Yuma said dryly. "Reckon I could locate that remuda again."

"Of course — while I provide that distraction in the rocks. Two separate areas of confusion, and the Apaches caught between. While they're still demoralized, our friends here can escape from the arroyo. Meet you at a predetermined place . . . and you'll have the necessary mounts."

"Leaving you stuck in them rocks holding off Apaches. If you're lucky, that is, and they don't get you straight off. They would after we was gone. They'd all be for you."

"Of course," Twill said calmly. "The idea is workable, don't you think?"

"Forget it. You ain't throwing your life

away that cheap, Mr. Twill. Forget it."

"My question was, will it work?"

"It's a damnfool notion. Christ, man. Any of a dozen things could go wrong."

"It's a chance, Mr. Pike. Just waiting, we stand no chance at all."

Twill unbent casually, coming to his feet, the movement briefly focusing Yuma's attention so that he failed in the first instant to see how Twill's long fingers as he rose stroked along the barrel of the Winchester beside him. And then suddenly his fingers circled the barrel and the rifle was coming up with him, his other hand whipping around to the lever.

Yuma was caught sitting down. Otherwise he might have countered the move in time. As it was, he had half-lunged to his feet, hand just touching his gunbutt, when Twill's rifle was leveled on him.

"Stop there, Mr. Pike!"

For the space of six heartbeats, the two men locked eyes.

"Man," Yuma said softly, "be reasonable. It can't work."

"It can. I'll kick up a hell of a fuss. Ride through 'em yelling and shooting. Before they can recover, I'll duck into the rocks and keep it up. Even the ones staying at their posts will be diverted. Perhaps just

196

enough —"

"Listen." Yuma took a step forward. "All right, I'll try for the horses, but you don't have to do this. Man, don't you understand? They'll get you! If they get you alive —"

"Don't take another step, Mr. Pike." Twill moved back a little, the rifle steady. "They'll get me. But not alive, I promise you."

Purdy and Roxanne were on their feet too, watching them. Twill wasn't covering Purdy, but he could bring the rifle to bear on him in an instant. Twill's face was hard, flat-planed, determined past all argument.

"Of course I don't have to do it," he said gently. "But your chances will be bettered by that much."

"Why?" Roxanne asked. "Can you tell us why?"

"Why, ma'am?" Twill was smiling. "Well, you might say it's Mr. Pike's example. He's shown me how to live like a man. Now I'll show him how to die like one."

"That's no reason," Yuma said harshly.

"No? Then try this." Twill's face smoothed to brown-black stone. "Here for a little while, I've been a man. I'm damned if I'll go back to being half of that."

"You can be anything you want."

"No. I can't, and you know it. I can't live your way . . . roughing it all alone. I'm not that kind. And there's no other choice for a man of color in that damned mean white man's world. No choice at all. If I go back and be the whole man I've been here, I'm dead anyway. Strung up by those white sheet fellows and my *cojones* cut off. That's the reserved treatment for uppity blacks. It is, you see, a highly symbolic act. A black corpse with its balls cut off is not even a dead man — just a dead nigger." Twill nodded slowly. "And they're right, you know — the white sheets. There *is* a difference. I can live like a dog back there . . . but I can never die like a man. *I can't go back, Mr. Pike.*"

Twill took a step sideways, glancing at Purdy. "Would you bring me the horse, Mr. Purdy?"

Yuma gathered himself and sprang, trying to drive head-on at Twill's middle, at the same time stabbing a hand blindly at the rifle to bat it aside. Twill swung aside just enough so that Yuma's head butted against his hip, and then he brought the rifle sweeping down. The barrel slammed Yuma at an angle across the shoulder and back, knocking him half away. He grabbed blindly at Twill's wrist, but he was half-stunned, his grip weak. Twill tore his arm free and swung the rifle against Yuma's head.

For perhaps a minute, perhaps longer, it

was all blackness. Then he knew that he was face down in the sand, red pain roaring in his head; his right shoulder felt paralyzed.

He climbed dazedly to his hands and knees, shaking his head. When his eyes focused again, he saw Twill standing a few yards away, regarding him patiently.

"I'm sorry. Are you all right?"

Yuma swallowed painfully. He nodded.

"Good. Then you can do your part — as I will mine."

Twill took the zebra dun's reins from Purdy and got awkwardly astride, fisting reins in one hand, Winchester in the other. Yuma climbed to his feet, swaying, watching him.

"Don't come after me, Mr. Pike. A meaningless bit of bravado: you'd get yourself killed and render my death quite useless. Mr. Purdy and the lady can hardly get out alive without you."

Twill started to turn the dun, then reined back, smiling, lifting the rifle in a sort of wry half-salute. "Don't feel badly, Mr. Pike. As I see it, there's not so very much difference between living like a man and dying like one. . . ."

CHAPTER THIRTEEN

Twill was gone. The darkness took him quickly and gave back a few flinty clinks: the dun crossing rock. The Apaches would hear, Yuma knew; they would pick Twill up swiftly. If he was lucky, maybe they wouldn't fire at once. But they might. They'd wonder why another fool-hardy *pin-da lik-o-yee* was trying to break out after the fate that the first two had met. And they'd be wary, wondering what he was up to, coming slowly through the rocks. They'd never guess.

Just maybe, for that reason alone, they'd hold fire out of curiosity — and give Twill his chance to sacrifice himself.

A sacrificial lamb. Our black sheep, Yuma thought. He was on his feet leaning against a rock, fighting the waves of dizziness. His head pounded from Twill's blow.

"You sure you can make it, boy?" Purdy asked.

"Have to." Yuma straightened. Some of the pain slid away, his brain was clear. "When he gets shooting, I'm going out. You two get ready."

"Where can we go?" Roxanne said.

"West. You see that star yonder, low above that bluff? Head for that, fast as you can. I can't tell you when. Wait till the ruckus is heavy and you judge the right time . . . just don't wait too long."

"What about the Mex?" Purdy asked.

"Cut his feet loose and bring him along." Yuma glanced at Tamargo. "If he gives you trouble, leave him for the 'paches. I don't reckon he'll give you trouble."

Tamargo's teeth gleamed. "You are a funny man, *muchacho.*"

Brush crashed on the heels of his words; Twill's yelling split the night. Then there was gunfire. Yuma said, "All right," and slung two coiled ropes over his shoulder, then picked up his bow and quiver of arrows. Roxanne caught at his arm.

"Pike, I want you to know. . . ."

She bit her lip; she shook her head. Yuma didn't know what to say either. He took her hand and held it tight a moment.

Then he was down in the brush going out through the break again. Not bellying down this time. Twill's diversion would have to provide enough cover; there was no time for elaborate stealth.

He went through the black tangles of brush and boulders bent almost double, not running but moving at a good walk, his senses trimmed fine. He had the Spanish dagger out and ready.

If he ran into an enemy, and he might before he knew it, he'd have to kill. In quickness and silence. A sudden encounter would give him no time to use the bow. The dagger — it had to be. That was all right. He felt best-armed with a knife.

Of course you had to know how and where to strike. The blade could be deflected by bone. On the other hand, a knife made no noise; it was easily kept clean and sharp, it was always ready. You could learn to unlimber and throw it as fast as you get out a gun and cock it. It was peerless at close quarters, particularly if you'd otherwise have to meet a bigger, stronger antagonist bare-handed. Something else he had learned, too: that most men, even those adept with fists and guns, were somewhat unstrung facing a man with a knife. If only momentarily, it seemed to drain the guts out of them; a split second could be crucial.

Twill had quit his wild shouting. But he was banging away steadily with the Winchester, and now the Apaches were putting up an answering fire. Twill must have gone into the rocks, abandoning his horse, and the Apaches would be pulling in around him. Alone, he couldn't hold them off long.

Yuma went faster, keeping low-bent but not pausing. So far he'd been lucky. He was outside the Apache encirclement and close to where he had detected the remuda earlier.

He halted.

A sound close by separated itself from the confusion of shots and yells; it sent a hot-cold ripple down his back.

He had heard it before, where Apaches had left victims. As a boy he had tortured small animals; he had watched his tribesmen work on captives. There wasn't always a lot of difference between sounds made by people and by animals in the extremity of pain. . . .

Yuma moved on.

He found the two horses first, sprawled where Apache bullets had cut them down. The Slaughter girl's body was close by. Her neck had been broken, apparently in the fall. Instant death. No sign that she'd been molested, nor had the body been mutilated.

Yuma kept going, but carefully. He was close to the horses, and the blind terrible sounds were nearer too. He mounted a shallow incline, then went down on his belly at the edge of a swale.

A man was nakedly spreadeagled below, his arms and legs fastened to stakes. His body was a gray blur under the lean moon; dark streaming clots marked where a half-dozen lances stood upright in him. Driven in, Yuma knew, with such consummate skill that no vital organ was pierced. It might have taken Severn all night to die. His shrieks that had torn the night an hour ago had dwindled to soft sawing croaks.

Yuma came up on one knee. The night ran cold against his sweating body. Go on, he told himself. Don't think about it. It's all you can do, so go ahead. He fitted an arrow, pulled the shaft whispering back to a tight string, and let go. It hit true: the croaking noises stopped.

Yuma remained where he was, listening. The remuda was very close: if those moans had been audible to the guard, their sudden ceasing would alert him. Abruptly, he heard the shooting stop. Which meant one thing. Goodbye, Mr. Twill. . . .

Now the Apaches would move back this way, Cipriano would suspect a diversion. Yuma rose and catfooted through the thin chaparral circling the ridge. Almost at once the dim moon showed a horse corral below: a crude frame of ocotillo poles that enclosed some twenty or so horses.

The guard was walking back and forth, rifle cradled in his crossed arms. Alerted by the firing, wondering what was happening, but sticking to his post. Yuma slipped down the dark ridge face, counting on the heavy shadows at this side to conceal his approach. The horses began scuffling and shifting; they'd either heard or smelled him.

The guard quit pacing. He froze in place, his head turning around and up. Yuma had an arrow fixed; he sent it winging. A clean miss, the shaft passing inches from the guard's arm. The Apache dropped to a crouch, cocking his rifle. Yuma straightened, knowing he was spotted as the rifle came up. Yuma palmed up his pistol and fired once, twice, seeing the Apache spin under the slugs' impact and go down.

The slapping echoes started the horses milling frantically. Cupping his hands to his mouth, Yuma let go with an imitation of a mountain lion's shriek. The horses surged in a panic against the corral poles, bursting and scattering them as they smashed through. Yuma was already lunging the last few yards downridge as the animals poured up the wash in a powdery haze of dust.

Running along the rim of the cutbank, Yuma watched his chance. A pony less alarmed than the rest was hanging back. Yuma sprang, dropping astride the animal, seizing its mane. He hugged its neck and drummed its flanks, clinging to the heels of the herd as he urged it on with savage yells. . . .

A gray band of light had grown along the sawtooth hills east. It had fanned across the whole sky by the time Yuma rode back southwest, heading for the cone-shaped bluff where he'd told Purdy and Roxanne to rendezvous.

He had pointed the remuda southward as it broke apart, afterward hoorawing the animals singly, scattering them as widely as possible. He had managed to run down and rope two of the less refractory animals. Using the spare lariat he had fashioned hackamores and leadropes; he was beaten sore, aching in every muscle, when the job was done. After several vain tries at catching a third horse, he had given up; time was pressing. Two of them would have to double up on one animal. . . .

He approached the dark hulk of the ridge; it loomed vast and deserted in a brass-colored wash of growing light. Yuma gave the whistling call of a quail. Brush crunched, and then Purdy and Roxanne were coming from the shelter of an ironwood thicket some hundred yards away. Ahead of them tramped Tamargo, hands still manacled behind him.

"Our luck is sure-hell holding," Purdy said, handing Yuma his Sharps rifle.

"For the time," Yuma said. "They'll be out

206

after them horses now. They'll be sure to pick up a few anyhow. Tubac's a goodly ways . . . we'll have to go some to keep ahead of 'em."

They rode west through the long day, wondering if it would ever end. The sun arced over them and past them; the blinding light puddled ahead of them in flat pools. At first they felt dogged by urgency, but the feeling deadened to a fatalistic acceptance after awhile: it was impossible, with one horse always double-burdened, to press hard or fast in this heat. Yuma and Roxanne, both of them lighter than Purdy or Tamargo, took turns doubling up on each of the horses. They changed mounts at each rest halt, which was almost hourly. The animals were hard to handle: it was tough enough guiding them with makeshift rope bridles, harder still to hold your seat bareback.

By the time the sun had westered low, they were deep in lava terrain that was ridged and canyon-broken. They rode in a cottony fog of exhaustion. The fierce heat had forced them to almost drain the big canteen. The one seep that Yuma knew of between the Tanks and Tubac was still a half-day's ride.

He had constantly checked their back

trail, alert for any hint of pursuit. But he couldn't see far across this shattered upheaval of land. And it was only now, watching their rear, that he saw the three Apaches swing into sight over a ridge less than two miles away.

They must have been the first to recover mounts. Not waiting for the others, they'd taken up the trail at once. A glance through his fieldglasses told Yuma they were driving their horses furiously, quirts rising and falling.

The sun had lost its glare, hanging like a bloated orange above the horizon. But hours of daylight remained. The Apaches were willing to kill their horses to overtake their quarry before dark. And the way it looked, they were going to make it. . . .

Yuma ordered a stop.

"You go on," he said. "I'm going to lay up for 'em."

Purdy ran a thumb along his rifle stock and spat. "Not alone you ain't, boy."

"You got to go on, Mr. Purdy. You'll be the bait."

They had halted in an irregular amphitheater that lay just beyond a shallow lava butte which temporarily cut them off from the Apaches. They'd come at a hard clip around that butte, Yuma pointed out. They'd see the party of whites a few hundred yards distant. And come on hellfire where, ordinarily, they'd exercise all caution. By then, Purdy, Roxanne and Tamargo would be close to that maze of canyons to the near west. Yuma would be hidden in place. And they would lead the Apaches in front of his gun.

"I ain't handing you any bowl of roses, Mr. Purdy. They start shooting, you could all be dead pigeons."

"Bait, eh? Well. . . ." Purdy spat again. "Man could be a sight worse, I reckon." He squinted at the sky, where the lone speck of a buzzard wheeled. "Like be a meal for that 'un."

"You ride along slow. When they spot you, move like hell."

Passing his reins to Roxanne behind him, he dropped off the horse and ghosted away through the rocks: black masses anciently veined with red from different lava flows. He reached the steep lift of a ridge and went up its blistered surface like a cat, wanting to get high enough for a clear shot. He hunkered down behind an abutment and slid his rifle barrel around its edge.

If he could drop two right off . . . that was his hope.

The Apaches swung around the low butte.

Seeing the slow-moving party of whites, they brought their quirts into full play and came streaking across the open. Yuma squared his sights on the chest of the lead Apache. The deep roar of the Sharps sent echoes bucketing through the rocks. The Apache was knocked spinning from his horse.

The other two reacted faster than he'd thought they would. Clinging flat against their mounts' necks, they put the animals into a pounding run for the nearest cover. The rocks were yards away, and Yuma, a fresh load in his rifle, followed one Apache in his sights and pulled trigger and missed.

By the time he'd thumbed in another load, they were at the rocks and tumbling off their horses. One man fell, rolling in the dust. The other scrambled behind cover. The one who'd fallen seemed to have trouble getting up. Then Yuma realized he was floundering painfully on his belly toward the rocks, one leg dragging.

It was Sus-to.

Yuma brought his rifle to bear on the crawling Apache, then let the barrel drop. Sus-to was no danger for the moment. Yuma fixed all his attention on the other man.

Suddenly the Apache broke out of the rocks, sprinting away to the left. Yuma fired, kicking up dust at the warrior's heels. Before he could reload, the Apache had achieved shelter. Not hesitating, he bounded away agile as a goat through more rocks, then was lost to sight.

What he intended was clear: to get up behind and above Yuma. Unless Yuma got off the ridgeflank fast, he'd be a sitting duck from above.

He went up the ridge quickly, scaling it at an angle, and then he was veering east along its summit. Sus-to's companion would show himself from this direction. A hot forest of fragmented lava littered the ridge. He wove through it, using it for cover, going carefully over rock polished to a treacherous slickness by the age-old action of wind and rain.

The Apache lunged unexpectedly into sight from Yuma's right: he had misjudged the warrior's line of ascent. Yuma came pivoting around on his heel; it skidded on lava that was weathered smooth as glass. His feet shot from under him and he went down hard, hearing the whine of the slug above him. The fall saved his life, but his whole body kept plunging down a slippery tilt of rock.

Clawing with both hands to halt his momentum, he lost his rifle. It clattered on for a few yards and fell down a short drop.

He almost went after it. Then his fingers found purchase in a pitted surface. Clinging with one hand, he jerked out his Colt with the other.

Temporarily he was cut off from his enemy. He heard the quick running pad of moccasins and suddenly the warrior was above him. He skirted the patch of slick rock with a bound, lit on firm footing and in the same movement swung the rifle in a tight arc toward Yuma.

Both fired. Yuma's shot hit the Apache in the face and exploded through the back of his head.

The warrior's slug hit inches wide, spattering rock particles against the side of Yuma's face. Half-blind with pain, blood streaming down his cheek, he edged sideways till he was off the polished stretch of rock. He scrambled upward on his hands and knees to the summit.

His ears rang; glittering sparks riddled his vision. As his head cleared, he became aware of shooting from down below: Purdy trading shots with Sus-to. Yuma began a slow descent of the ridge, clinging to the available cover so he wouldn't be a target for Sus-to's rifle.

But Purdy was keeping the crippled Apache occupied. Not knowing Sus-to was helpless, the driver had worked swiftly back on foot; he was raking the rocks where the Apache was laid up with a steady fire.

Yuma made a swift circle and came up on Sus-to's exposed side. Moving into the open now, he walked up on Sus-to from behind, halting perhaps twenty yards from him.

Sus-to was almost flat to the ground, firing between the rocks at Purdy's position. Hearing or sensing something, he squirmed partly around on his belly. He saw Yuma; he levered his Winchester furiously. Yuma cocked his pistol.

"Throw the *pesh-e-gar* away," he said. "I do not want to kill you."

Sus-to's face was a contorted smear of dirt and blood. "You killed me four suns ago, *sheek-a-say.*"

He started to bring the rifle up, and Yuma shot him.

CHAPTER FOURTEEN

By noon of the next day, they reached the seep. It was located in a dry wash at the base of Macklin's Mountain, a mesa-crowned peak which Yuma had used all morning to guide him. They made a noon halt on the sandy floor of the wash. Yuma knelt and began digging with his hands. He scooped down to damp earth, making a wide hollow. While it slowly filled with water, he hunted around for any edible plants.

The others rested in the shade of splintered boulders. The terrific heat was spongelike, soaking the vitality out of them. Purdy and Roxanne lay on their backs, eyes closed. Tamargo sat with his knees pulled up, looking altogether relaxed. His wrists, manacled in front so he could handle his horse, rested on his knees; his long capable hands hung loose. His eyes stayed the same as always: snakelike and restless.

They should reach the roistering silver camp of Tubac sometime after dark. Yuma (rarely an optimist) was starting to believe, at last, that they had a chance of making it. Depending on how close Cipriano was. Some of his men, perhaps most of them, had caught their horses and by now were long on the trail. Cipriano would lead them like a wolf on a high scent. Driving at a furious pace because he'd know the whites were close to sanctuary.

It was a crucial time for Tamargo, too. His chances for making a break were narrowing by the hour. He'd seize at the slightest chance. Deceptively relaxed, he was watching for it. And Yuma was watching him. He intended, if the Spaniard made one suspicious move, to shoot him.

Yuma distributed among them what little he found in the way of food. It was pulpy, almost tasteless fare; but beaten numb by heat and exhaustion, nobody had much appetite anyway.

Roxanne chewed on a fibrous bulb, grimacing. "My God. What is it?"

"*Tuna.* Fruit of the nopal cactus. Supposed to be edible."

"And this other stuff?"

"Squaw cabbage. Young shoots are best, but I couldn't find none."

"No wonder the whole U.S. Army can't whip the Apaches. If they can hold body and soul together on this, they're unbeatable."

The words had a dry edge. But she managed a smile. Managed it beautifully even with sun-cracked lips. Her skin was pinkly burned, her skirt and blouse in tatters. Looking at her, he thought back on that moment of passion at the Tanks. It had been like a storm that built slowly and broke suddenly, lashing them to an uncontrollable pitch. Neither had made any reference to it since. But the hot memory colored their thoughts of each other, making them careful in their talk.

Roxanne studied the backs of her sun-burned hands. "Twill," she murmured. "I'll remember that man a long time. What he did. You think he did it for us . . . a little?"

"I reckon. He figured we was worth it."

"I hope so. I just wish he hadn't had to die that way . . . not caring any more."

"He cared. He wanted to live as much as any of us."

"I guess he did."

Yuma glanced at the hollow he'd scooped in the sand. It was nearly full of cloudy water. He got the canteen and filled it and passed it to Roxanne.

"Drink all you can now. I'll fill it up again, then water the horses."

She drank and made a face. "I hate to keep complaining, but. . . ."

"Minerals. It won't hurt you. Some places it's so bad your jaw would tie up in a knot."

She handed the canteen to Purdy, then began to pace back and forth across the wash, rubbing the small of her back to work out the cramps. Yuma gave Tamargo the canteen and let him drink. Afterward he again filled it up and capped it, then led the horses one by one over to the water hollow.

Tamargo made his move suddenly.

Roxanne's slow pacing hadn't taken her closer than three yards to the Spaniard. But

216

it was enough. He uncoiled like a striking rattler and literally sprang. He hit her behind the knees and dumped her in a face-down sprawl and pounced on her. All in a few seconds.

Yuma was watering the last horse. He dropped the rope bridle and came wheeling around, his pistol out and cocked. It was already too late. Roxanne was pinned under Tamargo's weight, his knee grinding cruelly into her back, his chained wrists around her neck. Her spine was arched to a straining bow by Tamargo's hands: cupped under her chin and wrenching backward with an easy strength.

"One little jerk, *muchacho.*" Tamargo's voice whispered; his face shone like brown oil. "Just a little jerk . . . eh? Then her back breaks like a stick."

Roxanne's head was already twisted back at a dangerous angle. She raked her nails down Tamargo's hands, tearing red furrows. He grunted and applied a bit more pressure; she dropped her hands.

"The gun, breed. Throw it over."

Yuma hesitated, but only for an instant. The knotty power that corded the hands at Roxanne's throat said more than the words. *One little jerk.*

He let the pistol off-cock and tossed it.

The Colt thudded close to Tamargo's knee. His shackled hands blurred upward, freeing Roxanne's neck, then scooped down with incredible swiftness to the gun. He climbed to his feet.

"The key. I trouble you for that, eh? Drop it. Now your knife. Slowly . . . slowly. Ah. Your *cartuchera* now, the cartridge belt . . . now get down on your face. You, Purdy. The same."

Yuma stretched out on his belly. After cinching the shellbelt around his waist, Tamargo collected their rifles and examined each. He hefted Purdy's by the barrel, walked to a rock and smashed the weapon against it, destroying the mechanism. Walking over to the hobbled horses then, he deliberately raised Yuma's Sharps and shot one of them through the head. It folded down and died in a shuddering spasm. The two other animals shied a little; they stood trembling.

Tamargo patted the rifle and grinned. "This is fine gun, *muchacho* . . . I thank you." A few remaining shells for the buffalo gun were looped in Yuma's pistol belt. Tamargo thumbed one free and breeched it. "I will not waste these . . . even on you."

Roxanne had fallen face down in the sand. She pushed painfully up on her hands and knees. Tamargo walked to her, seized a handful of her hair and dragged her to her feet. He yanked her head back, jamming the rifle muzzle under her chin.

"I don't ask you, my beautiful. I tell you *Comprendes?* You come with me. You get on the horse and ride him. If you slow me, I blow your beautiful head off."

He gave her a stumbling shove toward the horses.

"You don't need her," Yuma said.

"Tamargo needs nobody. But it's good to have a woman along." He laughed and held the Sharps in one hand at arm's length, centering it on Yuma's head. "It would be ver' easy, breed. For you, too easy. There is your brother . . . eh? Maybe he will come soon. Without the horse, I don't think you get far."

Tamargo laughed again. His whole body rippled with a dry rollicking mirth. Jerking around, he walked to Roxanne and caught her around the waist. He lifted, half-throwing her astride one of the horses. Removing the hobble ropes from both animals, he tied one on her mount for a lead-rope. Then he slung the canteen strap over his shoulder and swung up on the other horse, gripping its rangy barrel with his knees.

He gave his sombrero brim a mocking tap with his thumb. "May all your luck be bad, fools. . . ."

They watched him ride southward, pulling along a skittish horse with a dazed woman clinging to its neck.

"Jesus," Purdy said. "He's crazy. Stark loony. How'n the hell far he expect to get like that?"

Yuma shook his head. "We better start walking."

"Tubac? We won't make it."

"Always a chance."

Purdy tongued his whispered cheek, resting his gaze on Yuma's hard-drawn face. "There's maybe a better way . . . I dunno."

"What?"

"How near Tubac are we?"

"I reckon twenty or so miles."

"All right." Purdy lifted his arm and pointed to the southeast. "Stage road makes a wide sweep north about there. I hazard we ain't more'n five miles from her walking that way."

"We won't get to town no faster."

"Nope. But say we come out on the road about ten mile east o' Tubac. There's a Mex fella got an outfit there. Raises truck and a few goats. Got a horse or two. Only place for miles. But maybe the 'pache scare's made him clear out . . . we could just lose time heading there. It's a gamble."

Yuma squinted at the shrinking figures of two riders starting a long rough descent toward the shimmering desert flats to the south.

"Let's take it," he said.

Tamargo had taken chances all his life. Nothing, in his view, was truly worthwhile unless a man filed his fate to a thin edge. But he was almost ready to admit that for once he had bitten off too much.

"Sangre de Cristo," he muttered.

The Apache horse had begun laboring under him, its tough wiry body shuddering with violent muscle spasms. He guessed what was wrong. This was the animal that Pike had been watering when interrupted by his play for escape. The horse had been ignored long enough to drink its fill. And now he had pushed the bloating beast too hard in the furnace heat of these flats. It was almost done in.

Nothing for it but to abandon it. And trust that he could achieve his destination on foot or by whatever conveyance fate provided. But *hijo de puta!* . . . this was scraping his fate finer than he liked.

He halted and dropped to the ground. He

uncapped the canteen, drank, and moved over to Roxanne Harris. This *gringa* had an admirable tenacity. She could still cling with both arms to her horse's neck though she was slumped across it, head hanging down. She moved slowly, lifting her face and pushing the tangled hair out of her eyes. Her face was reddened and puffy, her lips cracked: a line of dried blood streaked her chin where he had hit her when she had gotten briefly rebellious. Her glazed eyes smoldered with a greenfire hatred that hadn't diminished.

"You are a woman, my beautiful," Tamargo said with genuine admiration. He held up the canteen. "Drink. It will help you hate better."

She hadn't said a word in hours and she didn't now. Just took a deep pull at the canteen and gave it back to him.

"Now I walk. See, beautiful, I am the gallant, eh? I walk, you ride."

Leadrope in hand, he took up the trek on foot, leaving his animal standing where it was, its head down, wracked by slow spasms.

Ahead, still many miles to the south, was the broken blue line of the Santa Ritas. Sonora . . . ten years it had been. The price of an old murder still hung over him, but that was a chance to be taken. The Yanqui law would make this border country too hot for his health. Till it cooled somewhat, Sonora could better contain her erring son. *Dios!* He could already taste the good dark beer of Mexico and that fierce green sauce that went with the true tortillas. It would be good to be back. . . .

The woman. He would like to take her all the way with him if she'd only be compliant. But she had said she'd rather be dead. Well, he did not have to take her all the way. There was time. . . .

More rough country ahead. Touches of greenery here and there. It would make for hard traveling, but there might be water and game. He did not know this part of the country well, a fact that made him profoundly uneasy. By tomorrow, one day more at the latest, he would be in familiar country; then he could always get by.

The steady tramping sent flashes of pain up his ankles and calves. Quivering flakes of light danced in his eyes. *Jesus Maria!* This was no way for a horseman to travel. But the horse could not carry both far, and he was not ready — yet — to leave the woman.

From time to time he looked backward. The Apaches did not particularly worry him. Always a chance, if they'd taken up the trail from the Tanks, that when they came to where the tracks split, some might follow his. But Cipriano's quarry was his half-breed brother. And if Cipriano spelled out the sign correctly, Yuma would get his first attention. . . .

Tamargo chuckled. How could Pike and Purdy make it to Tubac? Purdy was leather-tough, but he was no longer young, and it was a long walk in this heat. Pike? He wouldn't leave Purdy. That son of an Indian whore's cross-grained quirk of honor wouldn't let him. Cipriano would find them both. . . .

The ridges opened up ahead, masses of red splintered rock stubbled with a sparse growth of catclaw and manzanita. Gravelly washes overgrown with bear grass and prickly pear running between the ridges. It looked anything but promising.

But almost at once Tamargo came on a clear stream in a vast wedgelike canyon flanked by steep-sloping ridges. The stream-banks were thick with scrub cottonwood and willows, and he flushed out a rabbit and knocked it over with a pistol shot. . . .

The sun cooled toward the horizon, delicately tinting the redrock heights. Reconnoitering upcanyon, Tamargo found a shallow cave high on its south wall. Cool and high-arched, with a dry sand floor. A comfortable place to spend a night. And a good lookout point from which he could see far down the canyon both ways.

Tamargo hobbled the horses in a well-grassed feeder canyon, built a small fire on a flat shelf outside the cave, and roasted the dressed rabbit on a crude spit. He divided it with the woman. The meat was tender and well-cooked, pulling easily away from the bones, eaten smoking hot.

Afterward, squatting on the ledge, rolling a stick between his teeth and studying the canyon floor below, Tamargo felt fed and satisfied. It was well, for he was in no hurry to leave. Why not lay over here tonight and through tomorrow's heat, and at nightfall take up his journey? He would travel only by night till he'd crossed the border.

As to the woman. Whether she came along or not was up to her.

She was sitting as far from him as she could get on the narrow shelf. Woman-like, she'd been unable to resist scrubbing away some of the grime in the stream, then combing out her tangled hair with her fingers and somewhat arranging her torn clothing.

"Ha," he said. "The beautiful tongue no longer wags. Tell me why is that. You run out of smart words?"

She turned that sea-ice look on him. "I have plenty. None you'd want to hear."

Tamargo tossed the stick away, got up and walked over, grasping her by the wrist. He twisted, forcing her to her feet. "Listen, *gringa* bitch . . . don't smart-talk Tamargo. I know your kind of woman. That breed — I think he had whatever you got and he didn't have to fight none for it. I think so."

"What if he did? He's a man. What are you?"

Her head was back, her eyes hard with challenge. He felt the heat of her body, the taut arch of her back under his arm which was tightly snaked around her waist. With a deep-throated growl, he drove his mouth down to hers in a grinding kiss. The fierce passion of her response surprised and momentarily diverted him. So that he almost failed to notice a subtle tug at his holster, the pistol coming out in her hand.

He wrenched the gun away and swung with his open hand, a flat hard staggering blow. He caught her again on the back-swing, this time knocking her down. She half-raised herself, pulling the back of her hand across her bleeding mouth.

"All right," she whispered. "Do what you want. I won't fight you."

Tamargo shook his head. "You had your

chance, my beautiful *gringa*. Get up."

She rose slowly to her feet.

"Go into the cave, *mi corazón*."

She walked in ahead of him. When the wall stopped her, she turned to face him, chin lifted, watching him. He gazed at her in the half-gloom: at the tall boldly curving body, the hot jade-colored eyes, the fiery stream of her hair.

"Dios," he murmured. "What a pity it is. You are so much woman. All woman."

He raised a hand to touch her throat, then curved his fingers down on the neck of her blouse and gave a savage yank. Cloth tore; buttons popped. He jerked again, the garment tearing free in his fist. She staggered and then caught her balance, standing straight, head up. Her body had an animal tautness; her eyes locked with his.

"I know you, my beautiful one," he said softly. "You cannot help feeling what you feel . . . eh?"

Heat-lightning in her green eyes. Pulse hammering in her throat. Shoulders and arms lovely in the gloom, like pale satin under dusk light. Those breasts swelling so proud and firm above the low camisole, a cleft of velvet shadow between them. He hooked his fingers in the top and tore the camisole down clear to the waist. . . .

CHAPTER FIFTEEN

Yuma sat at the crude and splintered table and wolfed down the meal that Ruiz' wife had set before him. It was good eating: boiled beans from the family truck patch, mixed with chilis and a thick cheese sauce and high seasoning. He mopped up the last of it with a hunk of biscuit and then leaned back, looking around at the cool low-ceilinged adobe room. It was clean and well-kept and made him conscious that his clothes were stiff with caked filth and that he looked and smelled and felt like a piece of green rawhide left too long in the sun.

Ruiz' children didn't mind. They stood by his bench hand in hand, a small boy and a small girl, both stark naked and brown as roasted nuts, looking at him with great lustrous eyes. He winked at them and glanced toward their mother who knelt by the fireplace stirring the simmering bean-pot.

"*Gracias,* Señora."

She nodded, a plump and worried woman whose pride and security was this small 'dobe house. She eyed him with a polite and bitter resentment.

"More?"

"No, ma'am, thank you."

He didn't blame her. Besides smelling of horse and leather and sweat, he had brought a shadow to her household. He represented the danger and turmoil of that outside world that she probably regarded as a constant menace to her few securities.

Ruiz appeared in the doorway leading to the small sleeping room. A gaunt and craggy man with a solemn mustache, he looked only worried, not resentful.

"Señor . . . your friend is awake. He asks for you."

Yuma swung off the bench and walked into the sleeping room. Purdy lay on the bed, his stocky weight sagging the leather-woven mattress stretched across a wooden frame. His face was sun-swollen and boiled-looking, all its lines etched with a deep exhaustion. His eyes were slitted nearly shut between the swollen lids.

"What'n hell happened?" he whispered.

Yuma settled on his hunkers by the bed. "You went off your head. Sun got to you."

"Yeah. I remember that. Reckon it was farther to this place'n I figured it was."

"Some. I hadn't no choice but to slug you . . . packed you on my back the rest of the way."

"Christ," Purdy said feelingly. His hand came out and gripped Yuma's arm. "We can't stay here. . . ."

"I told Ruiz that. Told him he best hitch his wagon and clear out for Tubac fast."

"Good. Time we did. . . ." Purdy started to lift himself; Yuma spread a palm on his chest and pushed him back.

"You lay quiet. They can pack you along in the wagon."

Purdy's stare was hard and inquisitive. "What you got in mind's something else, ain't it?"

"Ruiz has got a spare horse. I'm taking him."

"Jesus. Tamargo?"

"Somebody's got to."

"Sure, but not you. You're 'most done in your own self, boy. You been bucking without no sleep as long as I have."

"Longer." Yuma grinned a little. "While you was napping, I filled my belly. I'll dog it out all right."

"Christ, man." Purdy seemed to grope for the words. "Look, you done more'n any ten men already. I ain't forgetting about the Duchess, it's a hell of a thing . . . but he won't kill her anyways."

"He might. You don't know. Avila said he killed a woman."

Purdy grimaced painfully. "I'm thinking most about Cipriano. Plain luck he ain't caught up yet. When he comes, he'll track us straight here. Then follow your horse-tracks out. He'll keep after you. Only safe place you can go is Tubac."

"Ain't no denying that."

"Ain't no arguing it neither, not with you." Purdy grasped his hand. "All right. Luck to you . . . all best. Only wisht I could side you."

"You catch hold of something wet and ring-tailed in Tubac," Yuma said, "save out a bottle for me."

"That's a promise."

Yuma went out to the yard. It was late afternoon; the shadows of house and tack shed stretched long in the fly-buzzing heat. Ruiz was standing by his small corral, chewing his mustache. His horses were a couple of old ganted-up nags and one handsome piebald gelding. An ancient ore wagon stood alongside the tack shed.

Yuma walked over to him. "You want to get hitched up, I'll help."

"I don't know, señor . . . you sure the Apache is coming?"

"I told you. Anyway you must of heard Cipriano is out. Should of got your family to Tubac before this."

"Sure, the last stage that come through, they told us. But I thought maybe Cipriano, he would never come this far west. The woman and me, we talk it over, she don't want to leave." Ruiz sounded half-apologetic. "It's her home."

"Her home is you and them kids. You can always come back. Pack what personals you want and leave the rest. 'Dobe don't burn, and you can always come back."

"*Es verdad.* The woman don't think on these things, she just feels."

"I'll help you hitch up."

They made a quick job of hitching the two nags to the old wagon and piling in Mrs. Ruiz' more prized belongings, including metal utensils and good linen bedclothes. Yuma helped Purdy out to the wagon and made him roughly comfortable in its blanket-heaped bed. Afterward Yuma threw Ruiz' scarred saddle on the piebald horse. He also borrowed a blanket, a leather water bottle and Ruiz' battered Walker Colt, a vintage weapon whose frame was reinforced by rawhide thongs. Mounted, he rode over to the wagon where Ruiz, his wife and children beside him on the high seat, was taking up his reins.

"I'll bring this stuff back in good shape," he said. "And pay you if I can't."

"*No, es nada.* Don't think about it. *'Dios,* Señor."

Ruiz swung the wagon out west on the stage road, yellow dust boiling up from its wheels. Yuma watched it go, then turned the piebald horse eastward along the road. It was easier than backtracking northeast to where Tamargo had split away from them. He had gone straight south: his trail would intersect the stage road and Yuma could save a lot of time by picking it up from there.

He doubted that the Spaniard had much of a lead. Not while he was held to a lagging gait by tired horses with no saddles. The necessity of getting sleep would slow him; so would having a rebellious prisoner on his hands.

Yuma himself was as dead tired as he had ever felt in his life. How long had he been going on no sleep at all or brief snatches of it? He couldn't remember any more. One sure thing: he couldn't afford to face a dangerous enemy with his wits loggy from exhaustion.

Anyway he wouldn't get far before night forced a halt. But he could shave off a few brisk miles in the cool hours before early darkness. And be on his way in the gray of dawn. All he needed was a few hours' sleep and then enough light to track by. . . .

Tamargo came awake in the woolly halflight

of unrealized dawn. He woke like a cat, all his senses trigger-set and tingling. He didn't know why.

Getting up, he went to the cave mouth and looked out and studied the canyon up and down. There was nothing, but he felt oddly unassured. He went back and stretched out on the cool dry sand, folded arms pillowing his head.

His nerves felt gritty and restless; he wasn't accustomed to such a feeling. He would like to rest here through the heat of day and make his plans. But the inner restlessness continued to needle him, as if telling him to push southward without delay.

His stirrings had disturbed the woman; she moved on the cave floor. Her body was a white blur in the gloom, huddled in the shreds of her clothing. Her painful moanings had kept him awake till he had threatened her into silence. Before, he had beaten her into unconsciousness. *Dios,* what a wildcat — a wildcat of hate and desire. He fingered a long scratch down the side of his face. Ah . . . but it had been worth it.

Roused from a tortured sleep, she was starting up again. Making little mewling twitches of sound that came as regularly as the ticks of a metronome. He slid his pistol from its holster and cocked it. The noise it made was sharp, raw, deliberate. The moans stopped. He smiled. She was learning, she could be trained. Was it worth the candle, though? She was probably so broken up, there was no pleasure left in her. *Es barbaridaal.* He could not be saddled with an invalid. He squinted speculatively along the sights of his pistol. Would it not be simpler to just . . . ?

He sat up quickly.

What was that? — a ring of steel on stone? It was so faint he had hardly made it out . . . but sounds carried a long way between canyon walls in such a predawn stillness.

Rising now, he glided back to the cave mouth and peered upcanyon. There . . . movement. A horse and rider picking their way along the brushy streambank, moving in this direction. Tamargo got the Sharps rifle and crept onto the outside ledge and flattened out.

Let the man get closer . . . just a little. Then.

The rider was coming slow. A watchful man who looked constantly up and around him. He is looking for something, ready for it, Tamargo thought. There was a familiarity to the shape and set of his body. Without seeing his face, Tamargo knew.

It was Yuma Pike. He had gotten hold of a

horse, he had come this far.

"Ah, *muchacho,*" Tamargo said with admiration. He settled his cheek against the rifle stock and hair-fined his sights on the rider's middle.

It was a far shot and the light was still not too good. But he did not feel like waiting. He would take no more chances with Pike.

Suddenly Pike halted. Had he seen the black opening of the cave? It would be enough to make him wonder.

While he was still wondering, while his body hung steady in the sights, Tamargo fired.

The heavy bullet slammed into the piebald's head. Yuma simply plunged sideways with the animal's fall: he managed to leave the saddle as it went down. He crashed into the heavy willow growth which only partly broke his fall. Then he was rolling free of it, tumbling down the bank. He knew the round booming voice of the Sharps: its echoes still clapped furiously between the canyon slopes as he lit in the water. The stream was pebble-bottomed, only a few inches deep. He scrambled to his knees and hugged the bank.

He had seen powdersmoke smear that dark patch that looked like a cave mouth.

Just as he realized it was still visible from the streambed another shot came whipping through the willows, geysering water close to his legs. The shallow bank didn't even begin to screen him from the rifleman.

Yuma floundered upstream for several yards on his hands and knees. He flung himself against a gravelly cutbank. A third bullet raked its lip, showering him with dirt. Yuma balled his body to a crouch and shrank hard against the sliding earth. Tamargo was getting the range; only the vagaries of downhill shooting had spoiled his other shots.

Yuma was still barely out of sight. And Tamargo could shift position as he chose and still keep Yuma pinned behind the bank.

Yuma pulled Ruiz' Walker Colt from the waistband of his pants. It was loaded cap-and-ball; the powder would be wet now. The powder and shot pouches were in a saddlebag on the dead horse and he couldn't reach them. Making the weapon useless to him, even if the range weren't impossibly wide.

About two hundred feet upstream the creekbed was half-choked by gigantic rubble from an old slide that had littered the canyon floor from one side to the other. It was cover of a sort if he could reach it. From there maybe he could work higher and lose himself in the catclaw that flourished in heavy thickets from top to base of the slopes.

He scrubbed a grimy palm along his jaw. He'd be exposed all the way in his run. The buffalo gun was single shot. But he knew what just one bullet could do. It was that, though, or wait here for Tamargo with wet powder. The Spaniard would be watching for a sudden move; he had to gamble on how many moments it would take Tamargo to catch and follow him in his sights. . . .

Yuma lunged up and out from the bank. Both his feet skidded on the slick-pebbled creekbed. He swayed for balance an agonizing moment, caught it, then churned his legs high in a driving run through the foot-deep water.

He made a straining guess at the speed of Tamargo's reaction time: he veered suddenly to his right. The bullet whipped water so close, it threw him off-stride. He completely lost his balance, slipped on a submerged rock, flailed away his footing and went down in a headlong splash. Then he was up and running and he was in the rocks and going through them up the bank.

He dropped down against a sizeable chunk of crumbling granite a moment and edged his eyes around it. The canyon slope was dangerously open as far as the first thickets. He saw that much, and he saw Tamargo on his high ledge raising up to shoot again. He shrank down tight as the shot came. It exploded the boulder's rotted top, spraying chunks of granite all over him.

Now.

He raced across the canyon floor and upward. The increasing slope plowed away under his feet as he climbed. He stumbled twice before reaching the thickets. Bulling into them, he crashed through for a few yards and made no effort at silence. Then he was in deep cover. He stopped. The buffalo gun boomed. A twig clipped off by the slug dropped on his hatbrim. The bullet had gone feet high.

All right, Cayetano. Now the game is mine for a spell.

Tamargo was furiously breaking brush as he began a hurried descent of the slope. He wallowed through it blindly, striking for the place he had last heard Yuma. And Yuma slipped noiselessly upslope through the catclaw. He didn't need to see Tamargo to keep his movements pinpointed. When he was sure he had passed him, he cut quickly sideways to move above him.

Tamargo's crashings thinned away. He was canny enough to suspect that his enemy had

eluded him, and how. A few tentative crack-
lings suggested that Tamargo was trying to
emulate him. Then he had the sense to stop
altogether.

Silence now.

Tamargo was waiting . . . he couldn't be
sure whether or not Yuma was armed. That
would make him careful. But he had the
buffalo gun. He could confidently stay
where he was and wait for Yuma's next
move.

Yuma changed his direction. Angling back
downslope toward Tamargo's position. A
scatter of crumbled rock mingled with the
catclaw. He went across it with infinite care,
clinging to the pockets of brush and avoid-
ing the smaller rubble.

Then Tamargo was just below him, his
shiny leather clothing visible through the
lacy wands of brush. Squatted on his heels,
he was peering around. His back was toward
the upper slope. Yuma kept low as he glided
down behind him.

Ten yards from Tamargo's back, he broke
into a run. He crashed straight down
through the brushy wands.

Tamargo spun around. The Sharps swung
with him, its barrel angling up fast. It was
almost in line when Yuma hurtled full-tilt
into him. The Sharps went off. Bellowing so

close to Yuma's head he felt the powder-scorch of it sear his temple.

The collision slammed both men off their feet. Tamargo went somersaulting down the steep raw slope and Yuma came tumbling behind him, carried by his own momentum. They fell for yards, finally caroming into boulders that brought them to a stop.

Yuma was stunned. He lay where he was, face down, for some minutes. Moving by painful degrees, he spread his hands and pushed slowly up onto his knees. Pain knifed his side; blood from his nose dribbled saltily into his mouth.

Half blindly he swung his head, looking around for Tamargo. The Spaniard was a ways downslope from him, his long body twisted in a terrible grotesquery. His feet pointed uphill, his head hung down.

Yuma's whole body was one vast pounding ache. It was a full minute before he could muster the strength to half-crawl, half-stumble down beside Tamargo. He saw that the Spaniard's head had met a rock. His blood and brains dyed his crushed sombrero and the gray rock itself.

Yuma fell several times getting down to the stream. He lowered his body into the water, stretching out flat in the shallows. The early morning chill slashed into his cuts and bruises like fire. After a minute he was numb all over, and then he began to shiver. He moved his arms and legs, feeling as if they belonged to him again.

Dawn was a pearl blaze across half the sky. He left the stream and tramped up the slope dripping wet, his teeth chattering. He recovered his rifle, pistol belt and knife, and continued upslope to the cave.

CHAPTER SIXTEEN

Roxanne did not recognize him. Her skin was hot with fever, inflamed by welts and bruises. She was deep in delirium, moaning, and she cried out sharply when he touched her. At least three of her ribs were cracked. There wasn't much he could do except apply primitive poultices to ease the pain and draw the fever.

When he went down the canyon floor to hunt for a patch of prickly pear, he discovered the horses in the feeder canyon where Tamargo had left them. As he cut the spiny paddles from some prickly pear, he did some hard thinking. Horses meant escape. But only for him.

He couldn't take Roxanne with him unless he tied her on a travois drag. He could probably rig a crude one out of the materials at hand. But that could be a dangerous recourse . . . he just didn't know. He was only sure of fractured ribs, not of any other internal damage she might have suffered. Any attempt to move her might kill her. Anyway, held to a crawl by a horse drag, how far would they get before Cipriano caught up?

He could ride to Tubac and bring back help. But that would take two days. By now Cipriano would be only hours away . . . or less. Long before Yuma could return, he would find and search the canyon and read the sign of what had happened. He would find the cave. Even if not for Cipriano, Yuma couldn't risk leaving Roxanne alone for two days in her condition.

He had to stay with her. But all that meant was that when Cipriano came, both of them would die.

Returning to the cave, he mashed the cactus paddles between two rocks to make a poultice. As he worked, he went over the possibilities again. He could bury Tamargo, he could try to cover up what had happened here, he could pile brush over the cave mouth to conceal it. Clumsy devices that wouldn't fool Cipriano or his desert-wise braves for a minute.

That left just one fine-shaved possibility.

One as thin as his chances of bringing it off. He felt like a man carrying his life on his fingertips. But he was going to try it.

They came as the noon sun was blistering down on the naked rocks of the canyon. Seven grim gaunt Apache warriors on horses that had been ridden nearly to death.

Yuma waited on the canyon floor. His rifle, pistol and knife were on the ground at his feet. He knew they wouldn't shoot on sight — Cipriano least of all. That would be too easy a death for an outcast and renegade. His empty hands were loose at his sides, his weapons at his feet. That was enough passport for a parley.

The Apaches pulled up a little distance away, wary of a trick. Cipriano slipped to the ground and tossed his reins to a companion and walked forward.

Yuma hadn't seen his half-brother in years. Now that they were face to face, a flood of memory hit him with a savage violence that washed everything else from his thoughts. He felt a wolfish pleasure in the meeting. One way or the other, the old score would be settled.

Cipriano wasn't tall, but his barrel-shaped torso was so thickly quilted with muscle that he looked almost top-heavy, his legs spindly by comparison. His chest strained his calico shirt from which the sleeves had been hacked away. They couldn't contain Cipriano's arms, arms like oak trunks, corded with muscle, so long that the ends of his fingers reached nearly to his knees. His head was massive, his face square and brutish.

"Do you want to die?" he said. "It is too easy."

"No. I have the choice."

"You do not choose!" Cipriano slammed the words down like hammer blows. "Only a *Shis-in-day* has the right, white-eyes!"

"I am of the blood," Yuma said arrogantly. "I have the right."

The others began nudging their horses forward; they pulled loosely around the two. They listened, their faces hard and watchful. Yuma was pleased to see Es-ki-min-zin among them.

"You lie." Cipriano's lip peeled off his teeth. "I say that you lie. Your mother was a white-eyed bitch. You live as a *pin-da lik-o-yee*. I spit on your white blood." He spat.

"I am a warrior of the People. I have climbed to the heights and thrown *hodden-tin* to the winds. I have prayed to U-sen and the four winds. When a man does these things, the white blood is washed from his body."

It was true. They all knew it.

Es-ki-min-zin drew a finger down the side of his face, thoughtfully. "You have spilled the blood of the People, Gian-nah-tah. Never the blood of an enemy."

"That is not a true thing. Es-ki-min-zin knows that once in Sonora when the Rurales attacked our camp, I killed one with a rifle. I was twelve summers old and I killed a *nak-kai-ye.*"

Es-ki-min-zin nodded impartially. "This thing is true."

"Once I killed a *pin-da lik-o-yee,* a white-eyes who ambushed me and tried to rob me."

"Yes. You've killed our enemies. But you've spilled the People's blood."

"Apaches have warred on Apaches. *Bedon-ko-he* against *Ned-ni* against *Cho-kon-en.* Apaches have killed Apaches. I am a *Bedon-ko-he,* I have killed in war. Now I choose."

"There is a thing between Tloh-ka and Gian-nah-tah." Es-ki-min-zin laid the words down with slow softness. He was saying them to all the men and to each man singly. "The Law is clear."

He swung off his horse and moved to where Yuma's weapons lay, and picked them up. He balanced Yuma's Spanish dagger in his palm, then bent in a quick movement and stabbed it into the earth. He reached for Cipriano's knife. The war chief stepped back, clapping a hand over the haft, scowling.

"It is the Law," a big warrior rumbled.

Again Es-ki-min-zin reached, and this time Cipriano let his uncle lift the knife from its sheath. He drove it upright into the ground about a foot from Yuma's. It would be the Blood Right. As much as Yuma had let himself hope for. Thanks to Es-ki-min-zin: his authoritative voice had raised the right legalistic points to give a definite tip of the scales.

The Apaches pulled their ponies back, isolating the two men. They squared off, circling. Cipriano's face was like brown iron. He was Yuma's height, half again as heavy, nearly as quick. His reach was greater and his big hands were like vises. Their sheer power might crack a man's head.

One had to make the first move to snatch up a knife. In so doing, he'd lay himself open for a split instant. A broken second of time that could be fatal.

Cipriano lunged, straining every muscle as his long arm shot out, fingers splayed, to close on his knife haft. At the same time he swung a foot to knock Yuma's blade to the ground. Then his arm was sweeping upward and out for a savage cut. He grunted, barely springing aside in time as the savage kick Yuma drove at him grazed his temple. It was more or less a feint that let Yuma lunge in when Cipriano side-leaped; he scooped up his dagger which Cipriano's foot had only tilted.

Cipriano bored in on his side before he could fully turn. He twisted, arching his body: the blade shot in crookedly and sliced his shirt and seared along his ribs. He brought the hard curled toe of his moccasin against Cipriano's skin and then slashed at his head and missed as Cipriano went down, bowled over by his own rush.

He turned a clean somersault and bounced back to his feet and rushed again, swinging his blade in wide glittering arcs. Outreached, Yuma retreated, circling back and away. Cipriano was limping slightly from the kick, but he compensated by taking the whole offensive, crowding Yuma fiercely over the rough and treacherous ground. He was trying to press him to the edge of the cutbank or maneuver him into stepping off it. But his leg hampered him and Yuma was too fast.

As Apaches went, Cipriano lacked patience. Yuma knew it and waited for the move. It came. Cipriano driving in hard and fast, the knife suddenly reversed in his palm, cutting edge up, striking for the gut. Yuma deflected the blade with a thrust of his own, then pulled aside lightning-quick as Cipriano's powerful stroke spent itself in an empty sweep.

Still moving aside, Yuma cut at Cipriano's extended arm, plunging the blade in angularly and twisting it quick and deep, slashing the tendons, feeling blood spray over his hand and wrist.

The knife dropped from Cipriano's nerveless fingers. But he was already coming around as Yuma sprang in to finish it. His left hand closed on Yuma's forearm, freezing the knife. The powerful crush of his fingers squirted blue pain up Yuma's whole arm. Cipriano twisted with desperate bulllike strength, trying to wrench the arm from its socket.

Yuma didn't try to break the hold. He hooked his foot behind Cipriano's heel, leaned suddenly into him, tripped him and fell with him. They lit on the cutbank edge and plunged downward in an avalanche of chunky rubble. Yuma landed on the bottom. And found himself helplessly pinned in the shallow water by Cipriano's whole massive weight.

Then Cipriano's hold was slipping, his body going loose and even heavier. A red mist stained the water and widened. Yuma tried to move the hand that was trapped with his knife between their bodies, and couldn't.

He realized that Cipriano had fallen on the upturned knife. It had angled upward into his body, slashing the big trunk arteries.

The life had run out of him before Yuma could muster the strength to roll his body aside. He pulled his dagger free and climbed the bank and faced the silent Apaches.

"If Tloh-ka has a friend, if there is a fight between us, let him say so."

He wrung the words out with a hard-dredged effort. He could hardly stand. His side was streaming blood. If one of them should take him up, he'd hardly survive the first pass. They looked at each other and the silence ran thin as water. This had been no ordinary feud, and they knew it.

"It is finished," said Es-ki-min-zin.

It was the end of more than a family quarrel. Cuchillo's peace had been sealed at last. By the knife of one son, the blood of the other.

The Apaches dismounted. They got Cipriano's body and carried it to his horse and tied it on. All of them rode downcanyon flanking the animal and its burden. There would be a burial in a hidden spot. It would befit a war chief of the People. And no Apache would ever name the place. . . .

He stayed in the cave with Roxanne Harris through the day. He changed the poultices and gave her water when she was able to ask for it. By dusk, her delirium had passed, the fever had gone down. She could manage a halting whisper.

"I want to thank you and I don't know . . . don't know what to say. Isn't that a hell of a note?"

"Forget it."

"I never will. You stayed by me. No man ever did that."

He wanted to tell her not to make too much of this and he wasn't quite sure how he could. "You met some wrong ones, that's all."

"Oh shoot, yes. That's my featured talent. Pike, I want you to know. . . ."

But she didn't say the words. Or wouldn't. She lay under their one blanket and shivered a little. She turned her head to look at the fire he had built on the ledge, its dingy ribbon of smoke furling against the bronze sky. Finally she said, "Where will you go?"

"Nowhere for a spell. We'll do all right here till you can be moved. Then I'll fix up a horse drag. . . ."

"You know I didn't mean that."

He sat on his heels, shifting restlessly. His shirt chafed the shallow wound in his side. "I keep on the move. Never stay any place long and then I generally go far and fast."

"All right. That says it all, that's fine. Keeps me from being a damned fool about things."

"I didn't mean. . . ."

"I know. You just go your way and let others go theirs, don't you? I'm the same." She reached an arm from under the blanket and patted his knee. "Did you think I'd put a claim on you? Well, maybe I'd like to. Like to try. But you do deserve a heap better."

"Too hard on yourself."

"No. I know myself. Nothing's ever lasted with me. Oh, I like to fool myself that it's all the kind of men I've met. But I really think I pick that kind because I know it'll never involve a commitment. Nothing to tie my fancies down for too long. Well, I guess you'd understand . . . we're alike that way."

"Maybe."

"All right. Do you want to try it like that?"

He looked at her: at the long full shape of her under the blanket, an arm laying white and rounded on top of it, and her faint, wry, puckish smile.

"Like what?"

"Look, friend, I won't be such a broken-down specimen too long. There are lots of places a couple of people can be footloose together. All I'm saying is, would you care to try it that way? No promises, no commitments? Just the two of us for a while, and see what happens."

A hell of a lot was liable to happen, he thought. "Sure."

Beneath the blanket she gave a mildly pleasurable wriggle, then winced. "Where to first? Any ideas?"

"Tubac. I got a sort of promise from Mr. Purdy about a bottle."

ABOUT THE AUTHOR

T. V. Olsen was born in Rhinelander, Wisconsin, where he lives to this day. "My childhood was unremarkable except for an inordinate preoccupation with Zane Grey and Edgar Rice Burroughs." He had originally planned to be a comic strip artist but the stories he came up with proved far more interesting to him, and compelling, than any desire to illustrate them. Having read such accomplished Western authors as Les Savage, Jr., Luke Short, and Elmore Leonard, he began writing his first Western novel while a junior in high school. He couldn't find a publisher for it until he rewrote it after graduating from college with a Bachelor's degree from the University of Wisconsin at Stevens Point in 1955 and sent it to an agent. It was accepted by Ace Books and was published in 1956 as *Haven of the Hunted.*

Olsen went on to become one of the most

widely respected and widely read authors of Western fiction in the second half of the 20th Century. Even early works such as *High Lawless* and *Gunswift* are brilliantly plotted with involving characters and situations and a simple, powerfully evocative style. Olsen went on to write such important Western novels as *The Stalking Moon* and *Arrow in the Sun* which were made into classic Western films as well, the former starring Gregory Peck and the latter under the title *Soldier Blue* starring Candice Bergen. His novels have been translated into numerous European languages, including French, Spanish, Italian, Swedish, Serbo-Croatian, and Czech.

The second edition of *Twentieth Century Western Writers* concluded that "with the right press Olsen could command the position currently enjoyed by the late Louis L'Amour as America's most popular and foremost author of traditional Western novels." Any Olsen novel is guaranteed to combine drama and memorable characters with an authentic background of historical fact and an accurate portrayal of Western terrain.